All I Have to Give

All I Have to Give

A Christmas Love Story

MELODY CARLSON

Revell

a division of Baker Publishing Group
Grand Rapids, Michigan

© 2008 by Melody Carlson

Published by Revell
a division of Baker Publishing Group
P.O. Box 6287, Grand Rapids, MI 49516-6287
www.revellbooks.com

Printed in the United States of America

Library of Congress Cataloging-in-Publication Data
Carlson, Melody.
   All I have to give : a Christmas love story / Melody Carlson.
      p.   cm.
   ISBN 978-0-8007-1882-4 (cloth)
   1. Christmas stories. I. Title.
PS3553.A73257A76 2008
813′.54—dc22   2008007510

1

"Do you think Michael's experiencing a midlife crisis?" Anna mused as she dipped a serving bowl into the sudsy water. She and her younger sister Meredith were cleaning up after a Thanksgiving dinner that Anna had hosted for her extended family. It was the first time she'd entertained this many people at one time, but the meal had gone relatively well, especially considering twelve people had crowded into their rather small dining room. The food had been reasonably palatable, and the table, which was actually a piece of plywood secured to a pair of sawhorses and hidden beneath a tablecloth Anna had sewn, had been elegantly set. Although Anna was now rethinking her choice to use Great-Grandma Olivia's Meissen china. She hadn't considered that, thanks to the elegant gold-leaf trim, all twelve place settings and the numerous serving dishes would need to be hand washed.

"I think your hubby is too young for a midlife crisis," Meredith said with her typical skepticism. "I mean, what is he . . . like, thirty-seven?"

"Thirty-eight in January."

"Even so, that seems pretty young for a midlife crisis."

"Maybe he's mature for his age."

Meredith laughed as she carefully dried a platter. "Okay, what's really going on here, Anna? Trouble in paradise?"

Anna sighed as she scrubbed some stubborn gravy from a dinner plate. "No, we're okay. It's just that Michael has seemed sort of distant lately . . . but then he's been putting a lot of overtime into this new business, and, oh, I don't know—I guess I'm probably just obsessing."

"Meri?" Todd called from where the guys were huddled in the nearby family room, cozily gathered around the TV in their usual holiday ritual. "I hear the baby crying."

Meredith rolled her eyes at Anna as she hurried to dry her hands. "Todd hears Jackson crying, but he can't get off his duff and go pick up his own son?"

"And I'm guessing the womenfolk can't hear him."

"Not over the roar of that ball game." Meredith tossed the towel aside. "Sorry to bail on you, sis, but it is Jackson's feeding time."

"No problem." Anna ran some hot water into the sink, preparing for the next go-round. "I'll be fine."

"Want me to send Celeste in to take my place?" Meredith's tone was teasing now.

"That's okay," Anna said quickly. "I can handle it."

Meredith chuckled. "You just don't want to hear our sister-in-law going on again about how 'our big new house will be oh so perfect for a great big ol' Thanksgiving dinner.'" Meri even had the southern accent down just right.

Anna smiled at her sister, then nodded. She didn't add that she was also getting tired of hearing her sister-in-law complain about how none of her size-two clothes fit her anymore. "I can't believe I'm only three months pregnant and I'm going to have to go out and get maternity clothes," she had whined when she'd seen the pumpkin and apple pies Anna had made for dessert. What Anna wouldn't give for that kind of wardrobe challenge! It seemed such a small price to pay in exchange for a baby. But Anna didn't want to go there today. She also didn't want any more help in the kitchen. It was barely large enough for two people anyway.

She held the clean plate up to the window now, allowing the afternoon light to come through the china's translucent surface. "You can tell it's fine china when you can see daylight through it," Great-Grandma Olivia had told her more than thirty years ago, back when Anna was a little girl and had admired the lovely set. With pink rosebuds and gold-leaf trim, Anna couldn't imagine anything more beautiful. Of course, her tastes had changed somewhat as an adult, but she still felt honored that her great-grandmother had chosen Anna, as the oldest granddaughter, to bestow this treasure upon. "Glad it's you and not me," Meredith had admitted ten years ago when Anna had gotten engaged to Michael and received the china as a pre-wedding gift. "I'm sure not into pink rosebuds." Anna had appreciated the china even more when Great-Gran passed on shortly before her wedding. The sweet old woman had been ninety-six and still living in her own little house when she'd died in her sleep. Although saddened that Great-Gran had missed her wedding, Anna had thought it was a lovely way to go.

"I'll bet you could use a hand," Donna said as she came into the kitchen. Donna was Anna's stepmother, but she'd been in their lives for so long that Anna and her siblings had pretty much accepted her in the role of mom, although Anna still called her by her first name. "I didn't realize that Meredith wasn't in here still."

"She's feeding the baby. But you can dry if you want." Anna rinsed the last plate and set it in the drainer. "I'm going to start getting things ready for dessert now."

"It was a lovely dinner," Donna said as she picked up a fresh dish towel.

"Albeit a little crowded in my tiny house?"

Donna smiled. "You'll have to excuse Celeste. She's so excited about their new house and everything."

"Well, she can host Thanksgiving at her big ol' house next year."

Donna laughed. "Yes, I can just imagine Celeste dressed in silk and pearls as she stirs the gravy and balances her six-month-old baby on her hip."

"Meaning that David won't be much help?"

Donna frowned slightly. "I do wish he was a little more excited about becoming a daddy."

"I know . . ." Anna shook her head as she remembered her brother's negative reaction when Michael had toasted him and his wife on their impending parenthood. "I couldn't believe what he said during dinner."

"Oh, I don't think he really meant it." Donna reached for another plate. "It's just that David wanted to be married for at least five years before starting a family."

"I think he should just be thankful," Anna said a bit too sharply. "After all, it is Thanksgiving," she added to take the sting out of her words. Then she changed the subject, telling Donna about the Thanksgiving party that one of her room mothers had put together for her second grade class. "It was totally over the top," Anna admitted, as she went into detail to describe the fancy decorations and foods that had probably been very expensive. "But the kids actually seemed to like it."

"Where does this china go?" Donna asked as she set the last plate with the others on the countertop.

"Back into its crates."

Michael poked his head in the doorway from the dining room. "Need any help in here?"

8

"Sure." Anna turned the flame up under the teakettle. "You can help me get the crates and pack up these dishes and get them out of here."

"Nice dinner, Anna," Michael said as they walked back to the spare bedroom.

"Thanks."

Michael picked up a plastic crate, then paused to glance around the guest room. "You know, I've been thinking about converting this room into a home office."

"But where would we put company?"

"Well, I thought maybe the, uh, the *other* room . . ."

Anna bit her lip but didn't say anything.

"It has really nice light in there," he added.

Anna felt her throat tighten. "That's true, it does."

"And I thought if I had a home office, maybe I could work at home more. You know it's been hard starting up the new business, but if I could get set up at home, I could spend more time here. And I thought maybe I could repaint this room, like a dark blue or green or burgundy, sort of like a den or library, with some bookshelves. Maybe you'd want to use it too, for lesson plans or grading or whatever."

Anna brightened a bit. "That does sound nice, and dark paint would look good with the woodwork and crown molding."

"So maybe we should store your china set in the, uh, other room for now," Michael said as they carried the empty crates back to the kitchen. "It'll be one less thing to move out when I start to paint in there."

"I guess so . . ." Even as she said this, Anna knew she lacked enthusiasm. Still, she tried to process Michael's suggestions as she walked back to the kitchen.

"Want me to make coffee now?" Donna held up the empty carafe.

"Sure." Anna unzipped one of the many quilted containers, slipped in a china plate, and topped it with a circular pad to protect it from the next plate—just the way Great-Gran had shown her.

"Goodness." Donna paused from measuring coffee and watched Anna and Michael carefully putting the delicate pieces away. "I didn't realize that china was so much trouble."

"It's just that I don't have a proper place to keep it."

"You need a china cabinet, Anna."

"That would be nice."

"I don't know why you didn't just use your regular set of dishes," Donna continued. "They're pretty enough."

"Because this china is special," Anna said. "And I thought the family, especially Grandma Lily, would enjoy seeing it out again."

Donna examined a teacup. "I suppose so . . . but it's certainly a lot of work."

"I don't mind." Anna picked up a full crate and carried it back toward the spare bedroom.

"Let's put it in the other room," Michael said from behind her. "Remember?"

"Oh, yeah . . ." She paused, actually holding her breath as he balanced the crate on one side and reached for the doorknob. She hadn't seen this room for a while. Probably not since last summer when she'd retrieved a diaper bag that she knew Meredith could use, since her other one had split at the seams. And she knew Meredith had put Jackson down for a nap in here today, but Anna had been busy in the kitchen at the time . . . and now they were probably out in the living room with the grandmas.

Anna cautiously walked into the room, feeling almost surprised to see that it was just as cheerful as ever. The walls were still a warm buttery yellow, and the creamy white nursery furnishings—the changing table, crib, dresser, and rocking chair—were still in their places, although Meri had left a red and blue baby quilt behind. Anna had long since stowed the pretty pastel bedding and stuffed plush animals. It had been too difficult to see those cheerful baby items placed around the room . . . so expectant and waiting.

Michael set his crate down against the wall, then slowly removed the one that Anna was still holding. "I know this isn't easy, honey, but I've been thinking we should clear this room out," he said quietly.

She nodded, a hard lump forming in her throat. "I'm sure you're right."

"Maybe we could give the furniture to David and Celeste. I mean, despite how she goes on about how great they're doing, your brother admitted to me that he wasn't financially ready for this baby yet, what with recently getting that new house and all."

"Yes, that's a nice idea, Michael." She tried to feign enthusiasm as she ran her hand over the smooth surface of the crib's headboard, then picked up Jackson's bright quilt and folded it neatly, placing it under her arm. She remembered how she had carefully researched this line of infant furniture online, looking for the safest manufacturers available. Making sure that it was nontoxic paint, and that the railing posts weren't too far apart, and that there were no fancy knobs or things for a baby's clothing to get caught on. No, she would have no concerns over the safety of her brother's baby with this well-made line of furniture. Still, it was so hard to let it go—such a final good-bye to old dreams. And what about the possibility of adoption? Yet that seemed unlikely since their savings account was gone, plus they'd incurred a small mountain of debt when they'd "invested" in every imaginable fertility treatment available.

11

Anna was blinking back tears now, staring down at the ugly tan plastic crates that were now cluttering what she had once considered something of a sanctuary. "Do we really need to store the china in here?"

Michael reached over and put his arm around her shoulders. "I know it's hard . . . but we need to move on, Anna."

"I know, but I just don't like seeing the crates in here."

"Well, like I said, I want to paint that other room . . . and, as you know, we're a little short on storage in our little house, and I—"

"Fine!" She turned and glared at him. She knew she was being unreasonable, but suddenly she felt angry. Really angry. "Your old MG—a car that doesn't even run—takes up our entire garage, Michael. And whether it's raining or snowing or sleeting, I have to park my car on the street. But do I complain about that? Do I?"

"But, Anna, that's because it's—"

"It's just *fine*, Michael. You come and you go. You do as you please. You'll get your home office and you'll ruin this little room—this nursery that I—I love. Well, fine, it's just perfectly fine. Don't worry about me. Just as long as you're happy. *I'll be just fine!*"

Michael blinked and stepped back. "But, Anna, that's not what I want—"

"Excuse me, Michael, I need to go serve dessert now!"

As she turned and stomped back to the kitchen, she knew that she was acting totally crazy, not to mention completely out of character. She knew that she was being irrational, and if any members of her family had overheard her little tantrum, they would wonder what on earth had come over her. This was so unlike her. But for a change, Anna didn't really care what anyone thought. Let them wonder. Let them speculate. Maybe it was time she acted up.

2

As she got ready for bed, Anna still felt bad about her temper tantrum. Really, what had come over her? Maybe she was simply stressed. Certainly, it had been a long day. And she'd spent the previous afternoon, and late into the night, preparing things for Thanksgiving. Still, there was no denying that she hadn't felt like herself for several weeks now. She leaned against the bathroom vanity and peered at her image in the brightly lit mirror. Naturally, she looked tired. But who wouldn't be exhausted after a full house of relatives and a long day like today? And judging by the dark circles beneath her eyes, she was probably slightly iron deficient again. No big surprise there. Out of habit, she had taken prenatal vitamins plus iron for years . . . well, up until a few months ago when she just couldn't stand to see that *prenatal* label one more time. She'd promised herself to pick up a regular brand of vitamins but then had forgotten.

She leaned even closer to the mirror now, examining the gray hairs that seemed to be multiplying daily. Like her mother, she had been blessed with a full head of thick, dark, curly hair. And like her mother, she had been going prematurely gray since her late twenties. At first she'd tried to cover it, but then she'd heard that rumor about cancer being linked to hair dyes, plus Michael had insisted he liked her hair just the way it was. And so she'd decided to go with the flow, letting nature take its course, which was apparently the fast track. But didn't the Bible say that silver hair was a crown of glory? At this rate, she'd be glorious by the time she reached forty.

Anna reached for her bottle of Tums, noticing that it was nearly empty. Hadn't she just gotten it last week? But her stomach felt worse than usual tonight. Probably from too much rich food . . . although she'd tried to go light on dinner and hadn't even touched dessert. She popped a couple of the chalky tablets and even considered mentioning her stomach problems to Michael, just to hear his thoughts. He had a knack for distributing good medical advice. But he was probably asleep by now anyway. As usual, they'd already kissed and made amends—maintaining their promise to never go to sleep mad. But the truth was Anna still felt a little out of sorts over his comment about her needing to move on. That was easy for him to say.

Yet, as she brushed her teeth, she told herself that Michael was right. She knew it made perfectly good sense to turn their spare room into a home office. In fact, it was a great idea, and she'd probably enjoy the room too. As she flossed, she knew she would love to have him at home more. It seemed he'd been gone so much these past couple of weeks. Furthermore, she was well aware that the baby nursery had a great southern exposure and would make a delightful guest room. It all made total sense.

Except for the fact that she just didn't want to let it go yet. Despite that it had been nearly three years since she'd miscarried the only pregnancy that, with the help of modern medical technology, she'd actually managed to carry for almost six months, and despite that they had exhausted their financial resources as well as their limited supply of frozen eggs and sperm, Anna still didn't feel she was ready to give up. Good grief, she was only thirty-seven. Besides, she believed miracles could still happen. Well, at least she believed that on a good day. Today had not been a particularly good day. But tomorrow might be better. Especially if her stomach felt better . . . and if she could just get her energy back. As Anna applied moisturizer to the fine lines that had recently fanned out around the edges of her eyes, she promised herself that she would eat sensibly tomorrow, whole grains and fruits and vegetables, and she would go for a nice long walk with Huntley, their elderly beagle, and she would not forget to take her vitamins—prenatal or not. Although she wondered if the iron might aggravate her stomach even more.

For good measure, she popped another Tums tablet and hoped that it would do the trick. At first she'd assumed that these digestion problems were just a lingering case of a pesky strain of flu that had swept like wildfire through the elementary school last month. But now she wasn't so sure. And about a week ago, an old nagging fear had begun to gnaw at her again—tugging at the corners of her mind and trying to get her full attention. But she had put it off, telling herself that she'd think about it later . . . sometime when she wasn't so busy—perhaps during winter break, which was only a couple of weeks away now.

Anna rubbed lotion on her elbows and reminded herself that she was overdue for a gynecologist appointment, but after that last one—a year and a half ago—when Dr. Daruka had given her the hopeless prognosis on ever getting pregnant, Anna hadn't bothered to reschedule her annual checkup. She'd had enough doctor appointments to last a lifetime, and if she ever put her feet in those horrid stainless steel stirrups again, it would be way too soon.

She clicked off the bathroom light and went to the kitchen to make sure that Huntley had fresh water in his dish. He'd been slightly neglected today. She gave him a Milk-Bone, a pat on the head, and a promise for a walk in the morning, then turned off the kitchen light. But on her way back to the bedroom, she paused in the hallway, stopping to gaze at an old family portrait. Anna had been about thirteen when it was taken and nearly as tall as her mom, plus her feet had gotten big enough to wear Mom's shoes. Feeling rather grown up, Anna had been trying out a new eighties-style hairdo that made her head look enormous, but at the time Anna had thought she was styling. Meredith had been eleven at the time, smiling broadly to show off her shiny new braces that she would later come to hate. And David, at nine, was gangly with an impish look in his eyes. Mom and Dad were seated in front, holding hands and looking generally pleased about life, as if they had no idea what was just around the corner.

Once again Anna got hit with that eerie sense of déjà vu—that haunting feeling that history was about to repeat itself. Of course, this time it would be different. There wouldn't be three children left behind to grieve—only a husband and an aging beagle. She stared into her mother's dark brown eyes, so much like her own, and attempted to discern whether or not Mom had known the truth when the photo was taken. She'd been so urgent about getting everyone to the portrait studio that Anna had later been suspicious—as if there wasn't much time left and Mom had to get this shot while everyone was still able to smile . . . and while Mom still had a full head of hair. Anna's mother had been only thirty-six when the family portrait was taken . . . and thirty-seven when she'd succumbed to ovarian cancer just a bit more than a year later—only months older than Anna was now. A chill ran through Anna, making the hairs on the back of her neck stand up. She shivered and wrapped her arms tightly around herself, then realized that she was standing in the drafty hallway with bare feet and only a summer-weight cotton nightgown to keep her warm. Who wouldn't be cold?

She hurried to the bedroom, slipped quietly into bed, and wished she could warm her chilly feet on Michael. But she knew that would wake him . . . and then she might suddenly begin to talk—about everything. She might toss aside all inhibition and simply unload these things on him, dumping all her anxiety and concern, as well as Dr. Daruka's numerous warnings that Anna needed to watch out for that "genetic connection."

Everyone in her family had always acknowledged that Anna looked "just like Mom." But Anna's secret fear had always been that she and her mother had more than their outward appearances in common.

Everything in her wanted to wake Michael now. To sob out her fears and to feel his arms wrap around her as he assured her that everything was going to be okay. But tomorrow was a workday for him. And, she reminded herself, he had enough stress on the job these days. Building a new business wasn't easy—especially during the holidays. He didn't need her worries added to his ever-growing pile. Plus she knew that this kind of angst was always the worst at night. By the light of day, she would probably laugh at her silly paranoia.

3

Anna hadn't really meant to sleep in the next morning, but by the time she woke up, it was nearly nine o'clock and Michael had already gone to work. But right next to the coffeemaker, which was half full and still hot, he'd left a note saying that he'd be working late again tonight and that he expected to be home after eight. Then he'd added, "Have a nice day. Love, Michael."

"I intend to have a nice day," she said aloud as she poured herself a cup of coffee and picked up the newspaper. Huntley's tail began to thump, and she wondered if he remembered last night's promise to take him for a walk this morning. Well, she would keep that promise . . . as well as the others she'd made. With a three-day weekend to look forward to, Anna planned to start taking better care of herself. Sure, last night's panic attack did seem rather ridiculous in the light of day, but just the same it was a good warning to pay attention to her health. Then, after just a few of sips of coffee, she got that same uneasy twisting in her stomach again, followed by the feeling that all was not well.

Anna shoved the newspaper aside, went to find her laptop,

and set it on the dining room table that Michael must've moved back in here before going to work earlier. The table was an old beater that she'd gotten at a garage sale shortly after they were married. She'd painted it pale green and found some mismatched chairs that she'd sewn chair pads for, promising herself that someday she'd get a real dining room set—something worthy of Great-Gran's china. But, like so many other things, "someday" hadn't come.

Anna opened the laptop and turned on the power, then went back to the kitchen to heat up the teakettle. What she needed right now was a nice hot cup of green tea. It would be part of her new "get healthy" plan. But as she waited for her sluggish computer to get online and for the teakettle to whistle, she started to feel slightly panicky again. What if something really was wrong? To distract herself, she popped two slices of wheat bread into the toaster and went to the pantry in search of some orange marmalade.

She returned to her computer with her tea and toast and, seeing that it was now online, went directly to Google.com. Her topic was *ovarian cancer,* and as soon as she hit *search* more than seven million results popped up. She narrowed the search to include "symptoms," and the list shrunk to less than two million. Then she scanned for a website that sounded reliable and waited for it to open up. She knew this information should be familiar to her. After all, Dr. Daruka had given her numerous pamphlets in the past. Then again, had she ever actually read them? Or had she stuck them away to read "later" as she hid beneath a protective blanket of denial?

Anna felt herself growing more and more tense as she studied the list of symptoms. Her palms were sweating, and she knew that her pulse rate was increasing as she began to mentally check off all the symptoms that she'd been experiencing. Everything from abdominal discomfort and bloating to gastrointestinal symptoms like gas, indigestion, and nausea, to fatigue and even urinary problems. There was hardly one symptom on the list that she hadn't experienced. To make matters worse, she discovered that ovarian cancer was sneaky . . . because symptoms often didn't appear until the case was quite advanced. Not only that, but women who hadn't given birth were at a much higher risk. And the risk climbed even higher when family history was involved—particularly on the maternal side.

Anna slammed her laptop shut, then raced to the bathroom, where she barely made it to the toilet in time to lose her green tea and toast. With tears streaming down her cheeks, she stood over the sink, rinsing out her mouth and splashing cold water onto her face. She knew what was happening . . . history was repeating itself.

Unless she was overlooking something. Oh, it seemed impossible and too much to hope for. Especially considering all the times she'd been disappointed before. But what if this time was different? What if she really was pregnant?

Anna opened the small storage cabinet in the bathroom, digging past toilet paper packages and tissue boxes until she found what she was looking for—a pregnancy test kit. She'd almost tossed it out several times before, but doing that would have felt like giving up for good. Besides, there was still one test remaining, and one was all it took. Really, what could it hurt to just try?

After several minutes, Anna stared down at the used strip. Of course it was negative. Why should that surprise her? She wondered why she'd even bothered as she tossed the kit into the wastebasket. Then she took it out again. She didn't want Michael to see it and wonder about it. Instead she wrapped the kit in newspaper and took it to the trash can outside. On her way back through the kitchen, she paused at her computer again, then sat down to read some more. Although there were informative sites that boasted of new procedures and improved treatments, Anna felt a growing sense of doom and foreboding. It seemed obvious . . . She *was* her mother's daughter.

She picked up the phone and called Dr. Daruka's office but immediately got a recording. "Dr. Daruka will be out of town during the Thanksgiving holiday weekend. You may reach her on Monday during regular office hours. If this is an emergency, please call 911. Thank you."

"Right." Anna hung up. "911 . . . you bet."

Anna took a long, hot shower, got dressed, leashed up Huntley, and headed for the neighborhood park. As she walked, Anna attempted to pray. She wasn't a stranger to prayer, but, she suddenly realized as she struggled to come up with the right words to pray, she hadn't prayed much during the past couple of years—not since losing the baby. Oh, it wasn't as if she blamed God. She didn't. Not really. But she had wondered why he hadn't helped out just a little . . . Giving them a baby had seemed such a small thing at the time—especially in light of all the harder-to-resolve problems of the universe. It wasn't as if she'd been asking to win the lottery or to be handed a leading role on *Grey's Anatomy*. She had simply wanted a baby.

But then again, God had probably known that Anna was going to get sick like her mother . . . and perhaps he hadn't wanted for her to leave a motherless child behind. If her pregnancy had gone full-term, her baby would've been nearly three by now. A girl, Dr. Daruka had somberly informed her at the hospital. Anna hadn't wanted to know the baby's sex before the birth—she had wanted to be surprised. If it was a boy they were going to name him Edmond, and a girl would be named Olivia after Great-Gran and Mom. Maybe it was just as well that little Olivia was safely in heaven with her namesakes now. Maybe God knew that Anna would be with her baby girl before long.

Anna walked and walked around the little park. She circled it so many times that even Huntley began to slow his pace, glancing up at her as if to question this odd behavior. The poor old dog was going on twelve, and his stubby legs weren't as strong as they used to be.

"I'm sorry, Huntley," she said. "Am I wearing you out?" She paused at a park bench, and Huntley, obviously relieved for this break, stretched out on the footpath in front of her.

Anna sat there on the bench, looking up at the bare trees. Okay, if her worst fears were really coming to pass, what was her next step? Well, besides making a doctor appointment, and that wasn't even possible right now. She knew she needed to talk to someone, but she wondered how she could possibly break this news to Michael. He'd already been through so much with her—all those years of useless fertility treatments combined with all those desperate nights when she'd cried herself to sleep in his arms. She replayed all that he'd sacrificed for her since their marriage. How he had reluctantly gone into what he called "that nasty room" to "donate" sperm for her, or how he'd continued at a job he'd hated just to keep up their health insurance policy (mostly for her, since the private school where she taught had no coverage). Not to mention how he'd willingly emptied their savings and gone into debt—all in an effort to make her happy. Or at least that had been the goal. And now, after she'd given up on more fertility treatments as well as a baby, and he'd finally been able to quit the detested marketing job to start up his own design firm with his buddy Grant, she was going to tell him this? It was just too cruel.

That's when it hit her—they had no health insurance! Not

a speck! They had known it was risky, but it was only temporary. Michael had quit his job in August, and they'd decided to save a few precious bucks—money that was needed for the new business—planning to purchase a health insurance plan after the New Year. But by then it would be too late . . . unless there was no diagnosis. Okay, perhaps keeping her illness a secret might be considered devious or dishonest. She wasn't even sure. But, to be fair, she didn't know for certain she had ovarian cancer. In a way, she'd been jumping to conclusions since no professional had examined her yet. And surely they wouldn't be able to call this a preexisting condition without an official diagnosis.

Anna did some quick calculating, counting the weeks off on her fingers. January was less than six weeks away. Whatever was going on with her would simply have to wait. Most of those weeks would be vacation time anyway. And, really, what difference would it make in the end? Anna felt fairly certain that her fate was already sealed, and she cried as she walked home. And, although she may have been imagining it, she felt that Huntley understood what was going on with her. At the end of each block, he would look up at her with those big, sad eyes, and it seemed they were full of compassion—as if he was saying he was sorry.

By the time she got home, Anna knew what had to be done. She had to "buck up." And that's exactly what Dad used to tell her and her siblings in the months following their mom's death. Dad hadn't been very tolerant of emotional outbursts. He took the stance that what was done was done, and no one should carry on about it. And so that's what Anna would do about this. She would follow her father's example and pretend like everything was just fine. Not only that, she had to make sure—mostly for Michael's sake—that this was the best Christmas ever!

4

"You're putting up lights this year?" Bernice, the elderly neighbor from across the street, observed.

Anna forced a smile as she continued her attempt to untangle the strands of small white bulbs, stretching them out across the lawn. "Yes, I decided it was time to get back into the Christmas groove."

"Not me," Bernice said. "Ever since Harry died, I just don't have it in me to decorate much anymore."

Anna peered at the white-haired woman. "I'm sorry," she said with compassion. "Holidays must be hard."

Bernice nodded. "Particularly Christmas. Harry just loved Christmas. He didn't mind climbing on the roof to put up Santa and the reindeer and the works. Every year I was certain he was going to fall and break his neck, but he never did. And, oh my, the grandkids thought he was the greatest. I can still remember their eyes lighting up when they saw the house glowing from one end to the other. And the tree—good grief, Harry always had to get one that reached clear to the ceiling." She tossed her thumb back toward the contemporary-style house. "And we have twelve-foot ceilings." She sighed. "It was really something."

"Do the grandkids still come for Christmas?"

"Mercy, no." She shook her head. "They all have their own lives now . . . other relatives to spend time with."

"So, what do you do for Christmas?"

Bernice just shrugged. "Oh, I usually pop in a microwave dinner . . . watch a Christmas special on TV . . . go to bed early."

Anna frowned, suddenly feeling guilty for not having this conversation with her neighbor years ago. "Well, how about if you come to our house for Christmas this year, Bernice?"

Bernice's eyes grew bright. "Really?"

"Sure. We usually go to my dad's house for Christmas Eve and someone else's for Christmas Day. But this year I'd like to do Christmas dinner at home, and I'd love to have you join us."

"Well now, I'd like that. Thank you." She smiled. "Thank you very much. And you let me know if there's something I can bring. I used to make a very nice Waldorf salad."

"That sounds great."

"I'm going to run home and see if I can dig up the recipe this afternoon."

Anna laid down the last strand of lights. "And I think I'm about ready to get out the ladder and get these lights hung."

"You're going to do it all by yourself?" Bernice looked slightly alarmed.

"Well, Michael's very busy with a new business . . . so I thought I'd surprise him."

"Do be careful."

"Thanks, I will."

Anna plugged in the lights to test them. She was relieved to see that, other than a few burnt-out ones here and there, they worked. Heights had never bothered her, and once she got out the ladder and started hanging the lights around the eaves of their bungalow, she decided to climb to the peak of the roof and have a look around. She was surprised at how different things looked from that vantage point. She could see over fences and into neighbors' backyards. Some backyards, like theirs, were neat and orderly—everything in its place. Well, except for the strip of worn grass in Huntley's doggy run, but even that was fairly tidy. Others were messy and chaotic looking. Like the one a couple houses down with bright-colored plastic toys strewn all about—what she wouldn't give for a yard like that.

Finally her work was done. She couldn't wait until dark to see them really lighting up the place. It had been several years since they'd done Christmas lights, and Michael would probably be pleasantly surprised. Hopefully he'd remember this in years to come . . . when he, like Bernice, had to rethink the holidays and come up with new traditions. She wondered if Michael would remarry after she was gone. Part of her hoped so, and yet a part of her didn't want to share him with anyone.

In the house, she made a list of all the things she wanted to do for Christmas this year—all the things it would take to make this the best Christmas ever. Of course, her resources were pretty limited. Most of her salary, which wasn't a lot since she taught at a private school with a limited budget, was going to pay off their bills these days—trying to wipe out the debt that had accumulated during those despicable fertility treatments. And now, more than ever, she knew she needed to stick to that financial plan. If all went well, she might have the debt completely wiped out by the end of the school year. That is, if she could remain healthy enough to teach until June. She sure hoped so.

She tried to remember how her mom had been during that final year. Of course, she hadn't worked outside of the home, but even so, taking care of a husband and three kids couldn't have been easy. Always their house had been neat as a pin with homemade dinners every night, bag lunches ready to take to school, and even the laundry neatly folded and sitting on their beds when they came home from school. Anna marveled at this now. These were chores that Anna still struggled to get done herself, but she rationalized that a full-time job took its toll on the housework. Plus she hadn't really been herself this fall. And perhaps, if her energy continued to falter, she'd need to enlist Michael's help with a few of the household tasks—like laundry, which she abhorred. But not until after the New Year. And not until their insurance dilemma was settled and her diagnosis was certain. Until then, she would manage somehow.

So, although her Christmas to-do list was fairly long, she tried to keep it economical. Fortunately she still had a couple boxes of unused Christmas cards . . . only because she hadn't sent them out the past two years. And she'd already tucked away a few things she'd bought for relatives during the year. It was something her mom had always done, sticking away gifts for future holidays. Even after Mom had died, Anna's dad had discovered numerous presents all wrapped and ready for them. Sure, there'd been bittersweet tears when these packages were opened, but Anna always knew that her mother had meant well. She just wanted to do her best by her family. And that's what Anna wanted to do. She wanted to leave Michael with only happy memories of this Christmas.

She was pacing in the kitchen now, trying to think of what she could give him for Christmas—what was it that he really wanted? Well, besides a long, happy marriage and a child—two things that were out of her reach now. What could she possibly give him that he would thoroughly enjoy? What could she leave behind for him to remember her by?

Then it hit her. His little midnight-blue MG convertible. The same car she had complained about just yesterday, whining about how it took up all the room in their tiny detached garage. As if she'd ever use that garage anyway, with its funky old wooden door that wasn't exactly easy to open, let alone allow her to drive a car into the garage without hitting something. But right now the 1966 MG was sitting in there with a gray dustcover draped over it, like a ghost car. Michael had purchased the little roadster shortly after graduating from college, back before they'd even started dating. His plan had been to restore it to its former glory, but dating, work, life, and marriage had gotten in the way. Still, they had enjoyed the car for a while, during their courtship period and the first couple years of marriage. And then the engine had overheated and now needed to be completely rebuilt or replaced.

If only she could come up with a way to get Michael a new engine for that car. She could just imagine him driving it around—after she was gone—and remembering her. It was perfect. Well, except for the cost. She didn't know much about engines, except that Michael had said it was very expensive . . . and that they could not afford it. And so the car had just sat for the past eight years. Of course, Anna didn't know the first thing about cars or engines. But she knew someone who did.

"David?" she said when her brother answered his cell phone on the first ring. "This is Anna, and I have a car question. Do you have a minute?"

"Go for it. I'm stuck in traffic at the moment."

"You answer your phone while you're driving?"

"I wear a headset."

"Oh." She presented her idea for getting Michael an engine for Christmas.

"Wow, that's not going to be cheap, Anna."

"I know, but do you have any idea how much? Or where I'd go? Or any of that stuff?"

"Well, I'm guessing you could probably get a rebuilt engine for, oh, I don't know, maybe five hundred. But a new engine would be more. Then you have to pay to have it installed."

"Oh . . ."

"Want me to do some research for you on it?"

"Would you?"

"As long as you guys let me borrow the car sometime."

"I'm sure that could be arranged." Suddenly Anna got a lump in her throat as she imagined David and Michael taking the roadster for a spin without her . . . after she was gone.

"I'll let you know what I find out."

"Oh, yeah," Anna said suddenly. "I almost forgot. I still have that, uh, nursery furniture . . . and, well, since we're not going to have a baby . . . I thought . . ."

"Oh, Anna . . ." His voice sounded sad now.

"I mean, it's really good quality, and I know it's very safe. Do you think Celeste would be interested?"

"To buy?"

"No, of course not. I couldn't sell it. It would be a gift."

"Wow, that's really generous, Anna. I'll tell Celeste, okay?"

"Okay."

"And I'll let you know what I find out."

"Thanks, David. And, oh yeah, please don't tell anyone about the engine for Michael. Not Dad or Meri or even Celeste. I want this to be a complete surprise, okay?"

"My lips are sealed."

Then they said good-bye and hung up, and Anna just sat

there by the phone. She hadn't really thought about how all this might affect her family. They'd already gone through this once. She hated to take them through it again. Perhaps it would be best to keep quiet about it even after January. Maybe she could hold out until the end of the illness before she broke the news to them—sort of like her mother had done. She had no idea how Meredith would react. Ever since losing their mom, they had been extremely close. Even when they were teenagers, friends would comment on the fact that the two girls rarely fought. Of course, she and Meri would say it was because they were so different. Where Meredith was outspoken and extroverted, Anna tended to be quiet and shy. Somehow their opposite natures helped to glue them together. Well, that and losing Mom.

Anna looked down at her to-do list and quickly tallied up what it would cost to create what she hoped would be a wonderful Christmas. Not that Anna thought money could buy happiness. She knew better than that. But she did want to do all she could, whether it was food or decorations or gifts, to make this year truly special—and memorable. Of course, she knew her biggest challenge would be that expensive car engine. How could she make some extra money quickly? She considered tutoring, but it really wasn't the best time of year for that. She knew that some retailers were looking for part-time workers, but she'd have difficulty explaining something like that to Michael. Besides, spending time with him seemed more important right now. And with him working so much overtime lately, their time together had been diminishing steadily as it was.

Perhaps she should've told her brother that she would sell that nursery furniture after all. But, no, that just seemed wrong. Besides, she knew that David and Celeste's finances were tight just now. Plus it had been Michael's idea to share the baby furniture in the first place. It would be nice to see that pretty set put to good use, as well as kept in the family. She might've given the pieces to Meredith for baby Jack, but Meredith had already been set on a very contemporary nursery with sleek designs and bold colors. Meri thought that babies preferred bright primary colors, claiming that it increased their IQs. Well, no offense to her nephew, but Anna wasn't too sure about her sister's theory, and besides, she preferred calming pastels for baby nurseries herself. Still, what did it matter now?

Anna looked out the kitchen window to see that it was just getting dusky outside. It was that purplish-gray time of evening, with just a bit of haze in the air. Probably leftover smoke from a smoldering leaf pile. Anna knew it was the perfect time to turn on the Christmas lights. She went out to the porch and unceremoniously stuck the plug into the outlet, catching her breath as her house burst into cheery light.

She went down the steps and into the front yard to step back and admire her handiwork. Very, very nice. Happy and bright and inviting. She smiled as she wrapped her arms around herself to stay warm. There was a definite nip in the air, and she wouldn't be surprised if it froze tonight. Perhaps if this cold spell kept up they might even have a white Christmas this year. She sighed to think of how beautiful their little bungalow would look all lit up like this, with a fresh white blanket of snow all about. She imagined how sweet that front window would look with a tall Noble Fir standing in front of it, glowing with colored lights and her collection of old-fashioned ornaments—things that had remained in the attic the past two Christmases. Well, that would not be the case this year. Anna knew that she would do whatever it took to make this a truly remarkable Christmas.

5

"You want to get a tree *today*?" Michael frowned over his coffee at Anna. "It's still November."

"Barely." She set down her mug of green tea. "Monday is December 1." She reached for the calendar behind her just to be sure.

"Yes . . . but it's four weeks until Christmas."

"More like three and a half." She flipped the page and pointed out the day. "Besides, a lot of people get their trees right after Thanksgiving. Loraine Bechtle, a third grade teacher, told me they usually put theirs up even before Thanksgiving just so the grandkids can enjoy it that much longer."

"That seems crazy."

"Not to Loraine."

"But won't the tree be all dried out by Christmas? And what about fire hazards? Don't forget this is an old house, Anna."

"I know, Michael. You just have to take care of the tree correctly. Loraine was telling us about it last week. Did you know you're supposed to cut the trunk again before you put it into the stand? And then you simply make sure the water never runs out. She also suggested you mix the water with 7UP."

"7UP?" He tossed her a skeptical frown.

"Or Sprite . . . it probably doesn't matter which brand. But Loraine said that the sugar helps to keep the tree fresh."

He sighed as he set down the newspaper. "Look, Anna, I think it's great that you're excited about Christmas this year. And I'm glad that you put up the lights yesterday. I'd been thinking about doing it myself except that things are so hectic at work these days."

"I know you're busy." She smiled. "That's why I did it."

"And it's great seeing your enthusiasm about getting a tree. I have to admit that I've missed that. But the fact is, I really need to get some work done today. I plan to work at home, but it'll take most of the day to rework a design that has to be done by midweek. How about if we get a tree next weekend? We could even go to a tree farm and cut one ourselves."

She looked at the calendar. "That would be fun . . . except that Saturday night is the school Christmas concert and the dress rehearsal is at two."

"How about Sunday?" He looked hopeful. "After church?"

She pointed to the date. "The Christmas bazaar is that afternoon—remember it's a fundraiser for Darfur this year?" She shook her head as she realized that she'd completely blanked out that commitment over the past couple of weeks. "And that means I need to get some more sewing done sometime before then."

In October, Anna had agreed to do a craft project with her sister and their mutual friend Nicole Fox. Meredith had gotten a great deal on a bunch of willow baskets, which she thought would be perfect for mini picnic baskets. Anna had agreed to sew colorful napkins and small tablecloths, which were mostly done. And Nicole was providing sets of colorful plastic plates and utensils that she'd bought with a deep discount from her mom's craft store. They'd only put one basket together so far, but it had turned out really cute, and Meri was certain they could pull at least thirty dollars apiece for them.

"See," Michael said, as if this settled it. "We both have a lot to do during the next two weeks, so why not just wait and get the tree . . ." He paused to study the calendar, then pointed to Saturday the thirteenth. "Then!"

Anna felt her lower lip jutting out, just like one of her second grade boys after being informed that recess would be inside due to rain. "But that's not even two weeks before Christmas."

"Yeah." He nodded. "Perfect."

Anna knew that it was somewhat crazy, not to mention obsessive, to get all bent out of shape over when they got their Christmas tree. After all, they hadn't even gotten a tree for the last two years. But perhaps that was just the point. She wanted to make up for it this year. And less than two weeks was not going to cut it. "What if the trees are all picked over by then?"

"That probably won't happen."

"But why take a chance?"

He just shook his head, clearly exasperated.

"I just want this Christmas to be special, Michael," she said. "We haven't done much these past few years. I just hoped this could be, well, the best Christmas ever."

His brows lifted slightly. "The best Christmas ever?"

She shrugged. "Sounds corny, huh?"

"Or maybe just a case of bad timing."

Anna looked down at the table. She had already imagined

35

the two of them decorating the tree this weekend. She had even considered making popcorn and stringing it with cranberries, the way Great-Gran used to. And Michael could make them a crackling fire in the fireplace, and she'd make mint cocoa and . . . well, Anna just knew that she couldn't wait two long weeks before getting a tree. She needed it now. And somehow she would get it.

She stood, took her empty mug to the sink, and slowly rinsed it. "You go ahead and work today if you need to, Michael. I've got some errands to run anyway."

"You see," he said, picking up his newspaper again. "It makes sense to wait on the tree, doesn't it?"

She forced a smile and nodded. "Yes . . . very sensible." Of course, she didn't admit that just because it made sense didn't mean she agreed. Christmas wasn't something you celebrated with your head . . . but with your heart. And before the sun went down today, Anna intended to have a tree in the living room. Already she could imagine that sweet piney smell.

⸙

Anna tried not to indulge in self-pity as she drove by herself to a tree farm about twenty miles out of town. She had considered bringing Huntley but wasn't sure how tree farmers felt about pets. But she was determined to enjoy this—cutting down a tree would be fun. And wouldn't Michael be surprised. Besides that, it was a perfectly gorgeous day. Yesterday's overcast skies had completely cleared up, and although it was crisp and cold, the sun was shining brightly. She had brought along an old pair of boots and hoped that the tree farm would provide things like saws and ropes to tie the tree to the top of her old red Toyota. As she drove, she even started singing Christmas carols, really trying to get into the spirit of things.

36

Still, she felt slightly sneaky, and she missed having Michael along with her. But it would be worth it later . . . when they were decorating the tree together, sipping cocoa, and enjoying the fire. She would make sure to have the camera out and ready to go. She wanted Michael to have plenty of photos for later . . . happy memories for when she was gone.

The tree farm was busier than she'd expected. After hearing Michael going on about how it was too soon to get a tree, she'd almost started to doubt herself. But seeing the muddy lot nearly full of cars, trucks, and SUVs, she knew that it was probably a good idea after all. She walked over to an area where people seemed to be waiting. She'd never been to a tree farm before and wasn't quite sure what to do.

"The next wagon will be here in about ten minutes," announced an old man wearing overalls, a red plaid hunting jacket, and a Santa hat. "There's complimentary hot drinks over there by the wreath booth. Come get your ticket for a tree, then go ahead and help yourselves to refreshments, if you like."

Anna waited in line to buy her tree ticket and was slightly stunned to discover that an eight-foot Noble Fir would be $72.

"And, boy, are the Nobles pretty this year," the woman assured her. "Plus we're having a great deal on the wreaths when you purchase a tree that's more than fifty bucks. You can get a gorgeous evergreen wreath with holly sprigs for just an extra twenty dollars. Normally they go for thirty, so you save yourself ten bucks."

"Okay," Anna said slowly. Then she quickly did the math and realized that this little expedition, by the time she calculated in her gas mileage, would probably be close to a hundred dollars total. Still, this Christmas needed to be special. And by getting the tree today, she would have three and a half weeks to enjoy it. What was a hundred dollars compared to that?

She picked out a nice, big wreath and put it in the backseat of her car, then got a cup of cocoa, which wasn't very hot and tasted slightly watery. But she sipped it and pretended to enjoy it as she waited among parents and squealing children for the wagon to come and pick them up. She tried not to feel sorry for herself as she realized that she was the only person who appeared to be alone. Besides, she reminded herself, it had been her choice to come without Michael today. She smiled as she watched a pair of preschool-aged brothers playing tug-of-war with a length of rope until the younger one finally gave up and let go, causing the older boy to plunge backwards right into a muddy spot. Anna chuckled, but the boy's mother did not look amused.

By the time they got onto a wagon, which was loaded with hay and pulled by a pair of draft horses, Anna was feeling like maybe this had been a mistake. She sat on a corner of the wagon bed, observing the couples happily interacting with their children, talking about what kind of tree they wanted and who would get to use the saw and where would they go for lunch later . . . and she suddenly felt very sad. She fumbled for the sunglasses in her purse, quickly slipping them on so that no one would see her eyes filling with tears as she realized that this—happy families with children—was something she would never experience. She swallowed hard, reminding herself that at least she had Michael. If only he had wanted to come here with her today!

"This is the Noble Fir section," the young man who was driving the wagon announced. Anna and another family climbed down off the wagon, and, taking the handsaw that had been loaned to her, Anna made her way to a small sign that said "8 Ft." She tried not to watch the other family—a dad and mom about the same age as Michael and her, a boy who looked about the same age as her second graders, and a girl who was probably still in preschool. They had on matching red sweaters, and the parents took turns getting photos of them with the trees. But the best they could do was one parent with the kids.

"Want me to take one of all of you?" Anna said.

"Oh, would you?" the mom said.

"Sure." Anna went over and waited as the dad explained how the digital camera worked, although it wasn't much different from the one she and Michael had at home.

The mom arranged the kids in front of a tall tree. "If it's a good shot, we might use it on our Christmas card."

"Okay," Anna said. "I'll count to three and everyone smile big." So she did. And they did. And she thought it looked pretty good. "Just to be safe, I can take another," she called out.

"That would be wonderful," the mom said as she adjusted the little girl's stocking cap. "We really appreciate it."

Anna's eyes got blurry as she snapped the second picture. Still, it was probably just fine. "Here you go," she said, quickly handing the camera back to the dad as she replaced her sunglasses.

"Thank you so much!" the mother said.

"No problem." Anna turned, blinking back tears. "Happy tree hunting!"

Anna walked into the thicket of trees, going down one row and then the next, but without really looking at the trees. She mostly just wanted to get away from that happy family, wanted to block their smiling faces out of her mind. Finally, realizing that she might get lost in this maze of trees, she paused and took in a deep breath, then looked up at the clear blue sky. She stood there for a long moment, just staring up

39

past the branches and toward the heavens. "Why me?" she whispered to God. "Why?"

She stood there for several minutes, as if waiting for an answer, but other than the sound of some crows cawing back and forth not far off, all was quiet. Then she took in another long, deep breath and, getting her bearings, made her way back to the edge of the Noble Fir section, where she examined some of the eight-footers more closely until she finally decided on one that seemed to look just about perfect.

Of course, sawing it down turned out to be a challenge of its own. She hadn't counted on the thickness of the trunk or her lack of skill when it came to using a handsaw. She tried to recall if she'd ever cut down a tree before, then remembered back when she'd been a girl and had gone out with her parents and siblings to cut a tree from the woods a few times. And, since she was the oldest, her dad had finally let her use the saw. But that tree's trunk had been much narrower, and she'd had Dad there to help her. It had seemed easy. Still, she continued sawing, pushing the blade back and forth and trying to keep it from sticking. When she was only halfway through, she decided to try cutting it from the other side. Perhaps that would be easier. So she sawed and sawed some more, and then, just as she paused to catch her breath, down came the tree, flattening her smack down in the damp dirt.

She fought to push the tree away from her, and although she wished she could make light of her lack of lumberjack skills, she felt close to tears. She stood and brushed the dirt and debris from the back of her jeans, then picked pine needles from her wool jacket and even a few from her hair. She gathered up her purse and the handsaw and reached down to pick up the trunk of the Noble Fir. But it was much heavier than she'd expected. She gave it a hard tug, but it barely even moved. How was she supposed to get the tree back to the road where the wagon would be returning? And how in the world would she get the heavy tree on top of her car? Oh, why hadn't she saved this holiday errand to do with Michael? Why had she been so stubborn? Not only was it excruciatingly lonely getting a tree on your own, but it was downright difficult too.

She gave it a couple more tugs, then finally gave up and went to stand by the road. At least she could flag down the wagon, and maybe someone would take pity on her and offer to help.

"Where's your tree?" the mom from the photo session asked. She and her husband and kids were lugging an even taller tree to the side of the road.

"It was too heavy," Anna said.

"We can help," the woman said.

"Sure," the guy said. "Come on, kids, let's help the lady with her tree."

They all went back to where Anna's tree was lying like a fallen soldier, and together they carried it back to the side of the road. Along the way, they exchanged names, and Anna, feeling somewhat self-conscious for being alone on what it seemed should be a family outing, explained that her husband was busy today but this had seemed the best weekend to get a tree.

"Oh, I definitely agree," the woman said. "We always get ours on the Saturday after Thanksgiving." She smiled at her husband. "It's a tradition."

"And we make a gingerbread house too," the boy said, using his hands to show how big it was. "It's more like a castle, really," he explained.

"With a gingerbread princess," the little girl said, her brown eyes wide with excited anticipation.

41

"Wow," Anna said, "that must be fun."

"Do you want to help us make it?" the girl offered.

"Oh, no," Anna said quickly. "But thank you—I'll bet it'll be really cool."

"Where are *your* kids?" the boy asked with a furrowed brow.

"Marcus," the mom said with a warning tone.

"That's okay," Anna said, forcing a smile. "I don't have children . . . at home, that is. But I am a teacher." She patted Marcus's curly dark hair. "And I have twenty-three kids in my second grade classroom."

"I'm in first grade," he admitted.

"Well, you look old enough to be in second grade."

He grinned. "Yeah, I'm kinda big for my age."

"Oh, here comes the wagon now," the mom said. She seemed relieved by this, and Anna hoped she hadn't made the family too uncomfortable. She wondered why it was that many people seemed to feel ill at ease when they encountered someone who didn't have what they had. Maybe it was simply human nature—a protective intuition that someone might want to take what you had. Or maybe it was just Anna's overactive imagination.

She tried not to think about these things as they rode back to the parking lot. And when the young man driving the wagon offered to help her unload her bulky tree and then get it tied securely on top of her car, she didn't protest. Mostly she just wanted to get out of this happy Christmas place. She was tired of watching families, of feeling like a poor kid with her nose pressed against the toy store window and knowing that all she saw—all those desirable things— were not meant for her.

6

Michael's car wasn't in the driveway when Anna got home. So much for his "I'll be working at home all day today" excuse. Although it was possible that he'd gone to the office, where the big printer and other pieces of expensive electronic equipment were kept. Anna got out of the car and studied the tree still tied securely on top. Perhaps it wouldn't be too difficult to get down, what with gravity working with her. So she untied it and slid it down, laying it next to the car, then stepped back to admire her prize.

"Nice tree," Bernice called as she checked her mailbox.

"Thanks," Anna called back. "I cut it down myself."

"It looks very Christmassy against your red car."

Anna laughed. "Maybe I should leave it out here, although I was hoping to get it into the house at some point."

"Need some help?"

Anna considered her elderly neighbor's offer, then shook her head as she imagined Bernice stumbling under the bulky weight of the tree and breaking a hip. Anna wanted the tree inside the house, but not that badly. "Thanks anyway, Bernice. I'll wait until Michael gets back."

She went inside to see if he'd left a note. But all she found was his empty coffee cup and the newspaper still spread out over the dining table. She straightened things up, then went to the living room to make room for her tree. Her plan was to get everything in order and ready so that when Michael got home they could easily put the tree into place and begin decorating.

She moved some furniture around, freeing up the space in front of the window, then went up to the attic in search of Christmas decorations. Anna had begun collecting hand-blown glass ornaments even before she got married. She'd gotten off to a good start by adopting some of her mother's fragile pieces after Dad married Donna and she brought in her own style of Christmas, featuring a white-flocked tree and silk flowers in shades of pink and purple. Not Anna's favorite look. Anna preferred the old-fashioned ornaments that, lucky for her, neither Meri nor David had the slightest interest in at the time. Although if David knew their collectible value, he might see it differently now.

Anna removed the dusty cover from an old cardboard box, then carefully picked up a beloved Santa ornament from where it was snuggled down into layers of tissue paper. This was the very piece that her mom had said was the beginning of her own collection back in the sixties. She'd purchased it in Switzerland during a college trip, and somehow she'd managed to carry it all over Europe without breaking it.

What would become of these precious ornaments after Anna was gone? She picked up a snowman ornament and held it up to the faint light coming through the small attic window. Would Michael want to use them? Or perhaps Meri or David should have them, saving them for the next generation. Anna decided that she should put together some kind of will, saying who should get what after she was gone. Not that she had much to leave anyone. But some of the family things should probably be shared with her siblings and their children. Of course, she knew that neither David nor Meri would want Great-Gran's china. Meredith had never liked it much, and Celeste already had a very contemporary set of china that they'd gotten for their wedding.

Oh, well, Anna didn't have to resolve everything in a single day. Right now she just wanted to focus on Christmas. She picked up the tree stand and, upon closer examination, knew that it would be too small for that big trunk. One more thing to add to her growing list . . . which once again reminded her of their limited finances. Already she'd stretched their budget with what Michael might consider an extravagant price for the tree. Nearly a hundred dollars! But that was with that lovely wreath that she'd totally forgotten about in the backseat. Well, at least she could have that up before Michael got home. She couldn't wait to see it hanging on their front door.

Anna carried the boxes of ornaments down the steep attic stairs, pausing in the kitchen to dust them off before adding "bigger tree stand" to her list. Then she fetched the big wreath from the car and was even more pleased with it. At the tree farm it had seemed nice enough, sitting there among the others, but now that it was home, she could see that it was perfectly beautiful with its varied selection of lush evergreens and shining holly with bright red berries. Even the big red-velvet bow was perfect. Anna stood back to admire it. Really, it was the best wreath she'd ever hung on their front door.

Suddenly she remembered their first Christmas in this house, seven years ago. She'd just started doing the infertility treatments, and that, combined with the purchase of the house, had made finances tighter than ever. To be thrifty,

45

she'd created a homemade wreath using a wire hanger and tying on greens she'd clipped from shrubbery around the yard. The sad wreath had been slightly lopsided and limp, but better than nothing . . . until a strong wind, just a few days before Christmas, managed to dismantle it completely. All that was left were a couple of sad sprigs of pine and the crooked hanger. Well, this year would be different.

Anna grabbed her list and her purse and made a Wal-Mart run, where she found a big tree stand as well as some other Christmas decorations that were on sale. And then, with Michael still not home, she put many of the decorations up. As it started to get dark outside, she turned on the exterior Christmas lights, made a fire in the fireplace, lit candles, and even had Christmas music playing. The only thing missing now was Michael. After several unsuccessful attempts to reach him on his cell phone or the office phone, Anna was getting worried. But then she heard the front door opening.

"Ho ho ho!" Michael shouted from the entryway.

She dashed out in time to see him dragging in a Christmas tree. Not her tree, but another one. It was about the same height as hers, but not nearly as pretty. And it wasn't a Noble Fir.

"You got a tree?" she said in a slightly accusatory tone.

He looked disappointed. "Hey, I thought you'd be happy."

She held out her arms and sighed. "Yes, of course I'm happy. Except that I got a tree too. Didn't you see it out front?"

His brow creased. "You got a tree too?"

So she told him the story of the tree farm. And he told her how he'd noticed a Christmas tree lot on his way home and thought he'd surprise her. "But you don't like it?"

"It's a nice tree," she admitted. "But the one I got is nicer." She tugged him by the arm. "Come on outside and see it."

Of course, once they dragged the tree up to the porch where it was illuminated by the Christmas lights, he had to agree that her tree was much nicer.

"So, what'll we do with this one?"

"I don't have a tree in my classroom yet . . ."

"You do now."

She hugged him. "Thanks!"

"You're really getting into the spirit of Christmas this year," he said as they went back into the house and examined her holiday decorating.

"That's right. And I thought maybe you'd help me get that tree in here tonight." She showed him the oversized tree stand. "You just need to recut the trunk and—"

"Can't it wait until tomorrow?"

She shrugged. "I guess . . . but I thought it would be fun to decorate it tonight."

"I'm worn out." He kicked off his shoes and flopped into his favorite chair.

"I guess I can do it myself," she said. "Is there a saw in the garage?"

He sat up in the chair now, reaching for his shoes. "Okay, Anna, if you're that determined . . . I guess I can do it."

She could tell by the tone of his voice that he wasn't nearly as enthused about this as she was, and she was surprised he was doing this without an argument, but she just smiled. "And since you're being such a good sport, I'll go start dinner."

He turned and looked curiously at her. "You mean we're not going out?"

Saturday night was usually their date night, but Anna had already decided that she'd fix dinner at home tonight. An effort to economize after her big day of spending. "I've already got something ready to fix," she told him. "And then we can decorate the tree—that'll be more fun than dinner and a movie anyway."

"If you say so . . ."

By the time dinner was ready, Michael had managed to get the tree in its stand, and the two of them then wrestled it into the living room. "That is one heavy tree," he said as they stood back to see if it was straight.

"And one beautiful tree . . . don't you think?"

He nodded, then pulled a twig from her hair. "I hate to think how much it must've cost, Anna."

"Probably about as much as dinner and a movie," she said. "Let me get some water for the tree and then we can eat."

She quizzed him about work while they ate, asking him how long this crunch time of working late and on weekends was going to last. But his answer was vague, and she suspected that he didn't see an end in sight.

"Are you still glad you got your own business?" she asked. "No regrets?"

"We knew it would be hard to get it going at the start," he said as he took another serving of spaghetti. "But it'll be worth it . . . eventually."

She wondered. Now more than ever, time seemed very precious to her. And the idea of Michael putting in long hours was unsettling. "How long do you think it'll be before . . . 'eventually'?"

"I know the business seems demanding right now, Anna, but trust me, just one year from now things will be a lot different."

Anna swallowed hard and looked down at her plate. Chances were things would be a lot different. But not different in the way that Michael was hoping for. Anna looked back up at him, tempted to say something.

"I'm glad you decided to do all this Christmas stuff early," he said. "I know I probably seemed like a wet blanket earlier . . . but now I think it's just what we needed. I've missed Christmas in this house."

She smiled at him. "Me too."

After dinner, he willingly helped her to decorate the tree. And he listened as she told him the various histories of each of the ornaments. She made them big cups of cocoa and popped some popcorn, and although he helped to string some, she was pretty sure he was mostly eating it. Still, it didn't matter. This was more about making memories than anything else. And she knew, for her, tonight would always be special.

Anna felt her throat tighten as she sat there looking at the tree and Christmas decorations . . . at Michael and Huntley sitting next to the fireplace. It was picture perfect. "Are you crying?" Michael asked her.

She blinked, then smiled. "Just because I'm so happy," she said.

He sort of frowned, as if he wasn't convinced.

Now she forced herself to laugh. "And I'm sure my hormones are messing with me too."

He nodded as if he could buy into that. And Anna decided that it wasn't exactly a lie either. In fact, it seemed quite likely that her hormones would be playing havoc with her emotions from here on out. She remembered how her mother had been during that last year, often crying over what seemed like nothing. Dad had told the kids not to be too concerned, saying that Mom's ups and downs were simply a part of the illness. But then, he had played down a lot of things.

Sometimes Anna wondered if Dad had been in some sort of denial. Or maybe he had simply shut down his own emotions. Because even when Mom died, Anna never saw her father cry. And if she or her siblings cried occasionally in the months following their mother's death, Dad would scowl his disapproval, telling them to "buck up" and "get over it." He'd even said that their mother wouldn't have wanted them to carry on like babies. But Anna wasn't so sure. She thought that Mom probably would've wanted them to express their grief—she probably understood that tears were part of the healing process. And when Anna died, she hoped that her loved ones would cry for her. At least a little. After that they could move on.

7

"David said that he and Celeste planned to swing by our house on their way home from church," Michael said as he pulled into the driveway. "David wants her to see the baby furniture."

"Oh . . ." Anna nodded, trying to take this in. She knew she'd offered them the furniture, but suddenly she wasn't so sure she could part with it.

"I know it's hard." Michael took her hand and squeezed it. "But David sounded relieved that it might save them a few bucks."

"I know." She took a deep breath. "And, really, I'm fine with it. I like the idea of a little niece or nephew using those things."

Michael looked relieved. "And I like the idea of having a home office."

She squeezed his hand now. "So do I."

"That looks like them now," Michael said as a silver SUV pulled up.

"Wow, you've already decorated for Christmas," Celeste

said as the four of them went into the house. "Kind of early, isn't it?"

Anna shrugged. "Maybe . . . but I thought we could enjoy it longer this way."

"What a good-looking tree," David said as they paused in the living room.

Anna told him about how she'd cut it down herself and then been tackled by it. "It's a lot heavier than it looks."

"You went to the tree farm by yourself?" Celeste said with a frown.

"I know." Anna laughed. "I guess it was a little desperate. But we haven't had a tree for a couple of years, and I think I was feeling Christmas deprived."

"If I'd known she was that determined, I would've gone too," Michael explained. "But I was working."

"It's okay," Anna said. "It all worked out in the end."

"And it looks great," David said.

"Want to see the baby furniture?" Anna asked.

"Sure," David said, but Celeste just nodded with seeming reluctance.

"I'll put on some coffee," Michael said as Anna led the way to the nursery.

"Anna said it's really well made," David said as she opened the door.

"Oh . . ." Celeste said with a slight frown. "It's painted."

"Yes," Anna said as she ran a hand over the rail. "It's non-toxic paint, of course, with a very hard finish. And it's all solid wood underneath."

"But it's very old-fashioned," Celeste said. "I suppose it would be okay for a girl . . . but it seems kind of feminine for a boy."

"It's just a nursery," David said. "Who cares what it looks like? As long as it's safe and sturdy and—"

"I care," Celeste protested. "And I don't want hand-me-down furniture for my baby."

"But it's never even been used," David said.

"And you can put any kind of baby linens with it," Anna said. "If you guys are having a boy, just get boyish-looking things and—"

"I already had my heart set on another set of furniture," Celeste said. She turned and glared at David. "Are you saying I can't even pick out my own baby's furniture?"

"I'm saying that this will save us a few bucks," David said.

"But the set I want is designed to grow with the child. The crib can be converted to a bed, and the dresser doesn't look so—so babyish."

David leaned his head back and let out a groan. "And I'll bet it costs a fortune too." Then he turned and walked out of the room.

"I don't see why he's being so stubborn about this," Celeste said in a wounded tone.

"I think he just hoped to save some money."

"But we're talking about our baby. Don't you think our baby deserves the best?"

Anna sighed. "Well, of course . . ."

"I mean, you got to pick out what you wanted, Anna. And even though I don't like it, I'm sure this furniture wasn't cheap. And then you didn't even have a baby. I'll bet Michael doesn't get on your case over the wasted money."

Anna blinked and swallowed over the lump in her throat. "No, of course not."

"I don't see why David can't be more like Michael. It's like he doesn't even want this baby." And suddenly Celeste was crying.

Anna knew that she should hug her sister-in-law, but

everything in her wanted to just run from the room and escape her.

"David acts like I got pregnant just to aggravate him." She sniffed loudly. "Like he thinks I'm enjoying all this pregnancy crud." She pulled up her shirt to reveal the top of her pants, which were unbuttoned and partially unzipped. "It's not exactly fun watching your waistline disappear. Before long I'll be as big as a house."

Anna didn't say anything.

"You probably think I'm being really stupid, don't you?"

"No."

"I just want David to be happy for us," Celeste continued. "Is it too much to want him to want this baby?" She started crying even harder, and now Anna opened her arms and gathered up her sobbing sister-in-law.

"I'm sure David will be happy . . . eventually," Anna assured her. "It's just that your pregnancy has taken him by surprise. But trust me, I know that David is going to make a really good dad. And he'll totally love having a baby. He just needs some time to adjust to this whole thing. It's a big change."

"Well, he's got until May to get used to the idea," Celeste said. Then she stiffened slightly, and Anna dropped her arms limply to her sides and stepped back, feeling uncomfortable.

"Maybe that's why God designed a pregnancy to last nine months," Anna said.

"All I can say is that David better get with the program."

"So . . ." Anna glanced around her forlorn baby nursery. "It doesn't sound like you're going to change your mind about the baby furniture then?"

Celeste's brow creased as she studied the furniture more closely. "I don't know. I suppose if we were having a girl . . .

and if David refuses to give in . . . well, maybe it would be okay. I guess I could think about it."

"Right." Anna wanted to tell Celeste to forget the whole thing and that she'd changed her mind about giving it to them, but instead she just pressed her lips tightly together as she reached for the doorknob. "Let's go see what the guys are up to."

The guys were in front of the TV, already tuned in to a football game, and Anna knew it was going to be a long day. Eventually she excused herself to the kitchen to put together some lunch for the four of them. It was as much to escape Celeste as anything. And when Celeste halfheartedly asked if she needed help, Anna quickly declined the offer. Her plan was to make grilled cheese sandwiches and tomato soup. She knew it wasn't a very exciting lunch, but she didn't care.

"Need any help, sis?" David asked as he slipped into the kitchen.

"Nah," she told him. "As you can see, this isn't going to be a very fancy meal."

"Hey, you know I love this kind of thing." He plucked a dill pickle from the jar on the counter and took a big bite.

"Hopefully Celeste does too."

He sighed loudly. "Celeste doesn't seem to like much of anything these days."

"She said she'd think about the baby furniture."

David brightened. "Really?"

"She said if you guys are having a girl, she might be able to work with it."

"That'd be great."

Anna lowered her voice. "But she thinks you don't want this baby, David."

"I'm not crazy about the timing."

"I know . . ."

"But it's not that I don't want it."

"Well, that's how she feels. Maybe you could try a little harder to see her point of view."

"Maybe . . . but she could try a little harder too. Celeste is so self-centered sometimes. Like it's all about her."

"Maybe having a child will change that," Anna said. "She'll have someone else to take care of."

"She's already talking about a nanny."

"A nanny?" Anna tried not to look too stunned.

"Yeah. Sometimes I think that Celeste thinks we're made of money."

"Well, at least she's considering my hand-me-down nursery furniture."

"Thanks for that, sis. I really do appreciate it. You know what old Ben said, a penny saved is a penny earned." He glanced over his shoulder as if worried that someone might be listening. "Hey, speaking of money, last night I did a quick online search for that particular item you asked me about."

She looked up from flipping a sandwich. "Any luck?"

"There are some options out there . . . but they're a little spendy, Anna. You didn't mention what you can afford yet."

"How spendy are they?"

"You can get a new engine for about seven hundred, but it'll cost that much again—maybe more—for the mechanic to install it. I'm assuming you want it installed, right?"

"Of course." She flipped another sandwich.

"Okay. I just thought you should know. Do you want me to order one?"

"Not yet. I need to figure out some things first."

"Well, just let me know."

Anna carefully put the lid back on the butter dish. It was

from her china set, something that had been missed when they were cleaning up on Thanksgiving. "Hey, David," she said as she picked up the lid again. "You don't think Celeste would like this set of china, do you?"

David frowned. "Why? I thought you liked it."

"I do." She studied the delicate floral pattern. "But it's not very practical. It has to be hand washed, and I don't even have a place to store it."

"You want to get rid of it?"

"I don't know . . . I mean, I realize it's been in the family and—"

"It's yours, Anna. You should do whatever you want with it. And in answer to your question, Celeste would definitely not want it. Don't kid yourself."

"And I know Meri doesn't like it either." Anna sighed and replaced the lid.

"But I thought you liked it," David persisted.

"I do like it. But like I said, I never use it." Anna was thinking about what would happen to the heavy crates of china after she was gone. "And I just got to thinking that maybe it's worth as much as an engine . . ."

David nodded. "Yeah, it might be. I mean, it's a pretty big set, isn't it?"

"Twelve full place settings plus every serving piece imaginable."

"And it's in perfect shape?"

"Absolutely."

David put a hand on her shoulder. "Anna, you're breaking my heart here."

"Huh?" She peered curiously at him.

He shook his head. "I guess I'm just trying to imagine Celeste doing something like that for me." He laughed. "Yeah, right. Maybe in my dreams."

"Or maybe when you guys have been married longer," she said, although she wasn't so sure. "You need to remember that Michael and I have been together for more than ten years . . . and we've been through a lot. That makes a difference."

David still didn't look convinced. "But I remember you guys from the get-go, Anna. You've always been like that."

"Like what?" Michael asked as he joined them.

Anna slipped an arm around his middle, then smiled up at him. "Like in love," she murmured.

He pulled her closer to him and leaned down to kiss her on the forehead. "Yeah, so what else is new?"

"Is this a private party?" Celeste asked as she joined them in the small kitchen space. "What's going on in here anyway?"

"Just lunch," Anna said as she turned down the gas under the burner. "And it looks like it's just about ready too."

Fortunately lunch, with a somewhat caustic conversation between Celeste and David, ended relatively quickly. Then the guys declared the football game "hopeless," and Celeste announced that she and baby needed to go home for a nap.

"I need a nap too," Michael said as he closed the door behind them. "What did you put in that soup anyway? Tryptophan?"

"Yes," Anna teased. "I thought it would be a sure way to safely get rid of our guests."

"That Celeste," Michael said, shaking his head. "She's a real piece of work."

"Poor David." Anna headed back to the kitchen to finish cleaning up.

"I thought she was going to rip his head off when they started talking about the nursery furniture again. Made me wish I'd never suggested you give it to them." Michael rinsed a dish and handed it to her.

"I was tempted to rescind my offer several times today." Anna slid a plate into the dishwasher. "I mean, it's not that I want to be selfish . . . but I'd just hoped the nursery furniture could be enjoyed by someone who actually appreciated it."

"I know how you feel. But give Celeste some time. Maybe she'll come around."

"I guess . . ."

But the truth was Anna felt like she'd rather just sell the furniture to a perfect stranger now. And that way she could put the money toward the cost of Michael's engine. But then she thought about her brother again. For David's sake, she would wait on Celeste. And maybe they'd have a little girl. Anna could imagine the pretty white furniture in a pale pink room. Although Celeste didn't care much for pastels. Well, even a hot pink room would make the white furnishings stand out nicely. And David would certainly be happy with the compromise.

8

"I hate Christmas," Monica Meyers announced as the teachers gathered around the big table in the teachers' room to quickly devour their lunches. This was the only real break in their schedules and a time when they liked to let their hair down. Particularly Monica. She was a first grade teacher and sometimes a little on the impatient side, which made Anna wonder why she'd decided to become a teacher in the first place.

"Why?" Loraine asked. "I adore this time of year."

"For one thing, we have to do all these extra things at school," Monica pointed out. "The Christmas concert, the parties, the special Christmas crafts, and then we're expected to make gifts for parents . . . you know, that whole hoopla."

"Which is one reason I love teaching at a private school," Loraine said. "Christmas traditions are fading fast in public schools."

"But it's exhausting," Monica complained.

"I find it exhilarating," Loraine argued.

"And I agree with her," Anna added. "I already decorated and put my tree up, and I think Christmas is wonderful."

"See," Loraine said, "that's the spirit."

"Yes, but your children are grown," Monica said. "And Anna doesn't have any. But I do. And I do all this stuff at school, and then I have to go home and do it all over again for my own kids. On top of that, there are Christmas cards to send, which means another yearly Christmas letter, and the decorating, and buying gifts . . . Have you guys heard what the average family spends on Christmas each year?"

"How much?" Anna asked with slight interest.

"About a thousand dollars." Monica just shook her head. "And they say that it's probably even more, but people don't want to admit it. Furthermore, most average American families use credit to cover holiday spending. So they're just going further into debt."

"You're starting to depress me," Nina, a fifth grade teacher, said.

"I'm just telling you the facts." Monica crumpled up her brown paper lunch sack and tossed it into the garbage can.

"Well, I don't care," Loraine said. "I still love Christmas."

"I can see Monica's point," Nina said. "I mean, I have kids at home too. And it is tiring. It's like we have to do Christmas twice. Once at school and once at home."

"See," Monica said, "Nina gets it."

"If you guys really dislike Christmas so much, maybe you should consider teaching in public schools," Anna suggested.

Loraine laughed. "Yes, that would teach them, wouldn't it?"

"And people don't have to spend so much at Christmas," Anna said. "I mean, isn't it up to the individual to decide what's best? There are lots of homemade things you can do."

"Who has time?" Monica asked.

"Not everyone gets Christmas vacation," Loraine said. "I find that I have more time than most people during the holidays."

"And I don't think we've ever spent a thousand dollars," Anna said. Although, knowing the cost of what she wanted to get for Michael, she knew this year would be different.

"You know how I've made extra money for Christmas?" said Victor, the sixth grade teacher who usually couldn't get a word in edgewise when the women were going at it.

"How?" Monica asked.

"EBay."

"You sell things?"

"Sure. Already I've made close to five hundred dollars."

"What kinds of things do you sell?" Nina asked.

"Just stuff we don't need. Not only do I make money, I clear things out too."

"You don't worry about fraud?" Monica said. "I heard that sometimes people buy things and then scam you out of actually paying for them."

"There are ways to ensure that doesn't happen."

"I have a set of china," Anna ventured. "Do you think I could sell it on eBay?"

"I don't know why not," Victor said.

"What kind of china is it?" Loraine asked.

"Meissen." Anna described the delicate floral pattern and gold trim. "It's twelve full place settings and I don't know how many serving dishes. All in perfect condition."

Loraine nodded. "Do you know what you'd ask for it?"

"Are you interested?"

"I am."

"That would probably be better than selling it on eBay," Victor said. "Because you do have to pay for shipping and pack it so that nothing gets broken."

"Do you have a price in mind?" Loraine persisted.

"Well, I need to do some research," Anna said. "But I'd like to get at least, well, maybe fifteen hundred for it . . . if I could. There's something I really want to get for Michael this year."

"That sounds reasonable," Loraine said.

"Really?" Anna blinked in surprise. "You're still interested then?"

"Quite possibly. But I'd like to do some checking on the prices first. And then, of course, I'd like to see it."

"Naturally," Anna said, trying not to sound too eager.

"It may be worth more than you think," Loraine said. "And I wouldn't want to take unfair advantage."

"I actually have no idea what its value might be," Anna said. "But I can do some checking myself."

"Speaking of checking . . ." Monica pointed to the clock. "Two minutes until recess ends."

They scurried about, finishing their lunches and clearing things up, but as Anna hurried to meet her kids in the classroom, all she could think about was the possibility of Loraine buying her china set. And, although Anna didn't really want to let the pretty china go, she knew that Loraine was the kind of person who would love it and take care of it. After Anna was gone, what more could she hope for anyway? Now if she could just think of a way to find out what the set was really worth. Maybe David would know how to figure this out.

After school ended and her classroom was empty, she called David at his office. "I hate to bother you," she said quickly. "But do you know how to find out what my china set is worth? I might have a buyer for it."

"Easy breezy," he said. "But I don't have time to explain it to you right now. How about I email you some information later on tonight?"

"That'd be great." She thanked him and hung up. Maybe she was going to make enough money to get Michael his engine after all.

"Ho ho ho," Michael called as he suddenly appeared in her doorway, bearing, once again, his Christmas tree. "Anyone in need of some Christmas cheer?"

"Thank you," she exclaimed as she helped him set it up in the corner she'd already cleared out. "The kids will be thrilled."

"Well, I needed to head downtown for a meeting, and I decided to stop by the house and pick this up for you."

"A meeting?" Anna looked up at the clock. She'd been just about ready to go home. "Does this mean you'll be working late again?"

"Sorry." He leaned down and pecked her on the cheek. "We're still in crunch mode."

She sighed. "I guess I can get some sewing done tonight."

"Good idea," he said. "And don't worry, this overtime thing should come to an end in a couple of weeks. That's a small price to pay for what we're accomplishing."

A couple of weeks might seem like a small price to Michael, but Anna was looking at things differently now. Still, she knew that it was pointless to talk him out of it. Really, he needed to get this business solidly launched now. Besides, that might afford him more time to be with her later on down the line—perhaps when she would need him even more.

"Thanks again for the tree," she said as he was leaving.

"My pleasure. See you later tonight."

"Don't forget to eat something for dinner, Michael."

"Same back at you."

Well, Anna told herself as she drove home, perhaps she would use her evening alone to figure out the value of her china set. And maybe, if Loraine was really interested, she could get that engine ordered this week. She hadn't even asked David how long it would take to get the motor here or any of the details on how they would get it into the car in time for Christmas. Hopefully she could get it all worked out tonight without worrying about Michael overhearing her. Really, an evening alone wasn't such a bad thing.

Even so, it was hard coming home to a dark house by herself. It was different when she knew Michael would be home soon, but as she walked up to the door, she knew that wasn't the case tonight. Maybe she should get a timer for the Christmas lights. Wouldn't it be nice to come home to a cheerfully lit house? Well, at least it would be like that when Michael came home.

Anna's stomach had been a little better today. But she still had to pass on coffee at school. Even with creamer, it was just too acidic for her sensitive digestion. And now she didn't feel like having anything much besides soup and toast. If Michael had been coming home, she might've considered making homemade soup. But as it was, she was grateful to pour a can of chicken and vegetables into a bowl and put it in the microwave. As it heated, she popped a piece of whole wheat bread into the toaster, then turned on her laptop.

As she ate her meager meal, she checked her email and was pleased to see that David had delivered as promised. He'd listed several sites that would be helpful for figuring out the value of her china set, and by the time she finished eating, she realized that her set (if in excellent condition, which she felt certain was the case) might be worth close to two thousand dollars. But to be fair, one of the sites said that the value of antique china was determined by the market. If you had an eager buyer, it was worth more. If not, it was worth less. She wondered how eager Loraine would be, and how she would show Loraine the china without tipping off Michael as to her plan. Finally, she decided to simply call.

"Oh, I'm so happy to hear from you," Loraine said. "I just looked up your Meissen design online, and it's just what I'm looking for. It's absolutely perfect."

"Really, it's what you wanted?"

"Yes. It's so similar to a set my grandmother had that I was stunned. I literally had to pinch myself."

"What happened to your grandmother's set?"

"Oh, my aunt has it. And she doesn't even use it."

"Will you use it?"

"Only for special occasions . . . but, yes, I would plan to use it."

"I was surprised to see what it's worth," Anna said.

"Yes . . . I was a little surprised myself," Loraine admitted.

"One site suggested I could get close to two thousand for it."

"Yes. It sounds as if we visited the same site."

"And my brother found a set on eBay for $1,400. But it sounded as if that set had some chips, and some of the plates had scrapes and markings on them. I can assure you that my set is just about perfect."

"I'd love to see it, Anna. I mean, if you're really serious about selling it."

"I am serious. But here's the problem: I don't want Michael to know that I'm selling it. I want his gift to be a surprise, and if he knows I've sold my china, well, he would probably get suspicious."

"Oh, I understand completely."

"And he's not here this evening . . . but I'm not sure when he's coming home. I mean, I'd hate to get it all set out and have him walk in."

"Yes. That wouldn't be good."

"I could bring it over to your house," Anna suggested.

"You wouldn't mind?"

"No. In fact, the timing might be good for sneaking it out of here without him knowing."

"Oh, that would be wonderful, Anna." Loraine gave her directions.

"Okay, I'd better hurry," Anna said. "It'll take me awhile to get it all loaded into the car. I assume you'll want to see all the pieces?"

"You might as well bring them, Anna. My guess is that I'll be writing you a check tonight anyway."

Anna was so excited that she had to remind herself to be careful as she carried the crates through the house and down the stairs. One misstep and she could ruin this whole plan. But finally they were all loaded into her car and she was driving across town to what turned out to be a very nice neighborhood. One of those old and established areas where the trees were big and the houses were beautiful. Loraine's house turned out to be a Queen Anne Victorian on a corner. What a great match for this set of china!

Anna carried one of the boxes up to the door with her, and then both Loraine and her husband Rich helped to carry the crates into the house. Soon they had unpacked enough place settings to set the large cherry dining table in Loraine's high-ceilinged dining room.

"Oh, they are exquisite," Loraine gushed. She turned and looked at her husband. "Don't you think so too?"

"I think that if you like them, I like them." He smiled. "Merry Christmas."

"What a wonderful Christmas present," Anna said.

"Well, Loraine's been pining after her grandmother's dishes ever since we got married more than thirty years ago. I even tried to buy them from her aunt several times, but nothing doing."

"And they really do look perfect in your home," Anna said. She sort of laughed. "Much better than they looked in my small bungalow. I didn't even have a place to keep them— besides in the crates."

"And they really do deserve a place of honor," Loraine said. She showed Anna the cherry china cabinet that matched the table.

"What will you do with those dishes?"

"Those will be my younger daughter's wedding present in June."

"Katy is going to be over the moon," Rich said.

"Now, Erika—that's my older daughter—she'll probably want me to leave this set to her," Loraine said as she held up a fragile plate, allowing the light from the chandelier to glow through it.

Anna swallowed hard against the lump that was suddenly growing in her throat. How she had longed to pass these dishes down to her own daughter someday. Of course, that was a dream that wasn't meant to come true. A dream she needed to forget about.

"You really don't mind letting them go?" Loraine asked as she set the plate back down. "You don't think you'll regret this decision later on?"

"No," Anna said firmly. "I want to do this for Michael." Then she explained about his little MG and how it had been sitting in the garage for so long.

"Wow," Rich said. "I wouldn't mind getting my hands on

a car like that. Say, if your husband decides he wants to sell—"

"No way," Anna said. "He adores that car. In fact, I do too. And once it's running, I doubt that he'll ever want to get rid of it."

Rich nodded. "Understandable." Then he pulled out his checkbook and wrote out a check for $2,000.

"Oh, I was only going to ask for $1,800," Anna said when he handed it to her.

"These dishes are in mint condition," Loraine said. "Two thousand dollars is a good deal."

"You're sure?" Anna tried not to stare at the check.

"Absolutely. And I can't wait to serve Christmas dinner on them."

"Well, thank you." Anna slipped the check into her purse.

"Thank *you*!" Loraine said.

Anna knew she should be happy as she drove home. And for the most part she was, although she knew she would miss her dishes. Still, she could hardly believe that not only had she made enough to buy an engine, but she also had enough to pay to get it installed. She couldn't wait to give David the green light on this thing. Hopefully it would work out that the MG would be ready to roll in time for Christmas!

9

As it turned out, David got so busy that he didn't order the engine until Thursday. "And it could take up to three weeks for delivery," he informed her.

"Three weeks?" she cried. "That could be *after* Christmas."

"I know."

"Isn't there a way to rush it?"

"I asked and they said it could get here before Christmas, but that this is a hard time of year to make promises on deliveries. I emailed you a photo of the engine, though. I thought if nothing else, you could print that out and put it in a card for him."

Anna knew it was unreasonable to feel so disappointed, but she did. She had wanted this to go perfectly. "I suppose I could do that . . . but I'd really hoped to have the engine in the car by then."

"Well, that's not very realistic, Anna." He'd already explained that getting a mechanic to install an engine just days before Christmas was pretty unlikely.

"Yes, I'm starting to see that now."

"But I did get another idea for you," he said. "You could get Michael a gift certificate from British Motors and make an appointment to get the installation right after Christmas. I talked to my friend Ron this morning—remember I told you about him, he owns British Motors—anyway, he said that he might be able to get the engine put in for you by New Year's if you get it scheduled now."

"New Year's?" She considered Michael taking her out in the sporty little car on New Year's Eve and smiled. "That might be okay . . . although I'd really counted on having the car all ready to go for Christmas."

"The main thing is that you're doing this, Anna." David sighed. "Seriously, Michael is one lucky dude."

Anna knew that her brother was thinking about his own wife. She could hear the defeated tone of his voice. "How's Celeste doing?" she asked. "Has she said anything about my nursery furniture yet?"

"I think she's still pouting."

"Oh . . ."

"Sounds like we'll find out whether the baby's a girl or a boy the week after Christmas."

"That'll be nice. Do you have a preference?"

He laughed. "Just whatever will make my wife happiest."

"What does she want?"

"Depends on her mood. If she's mad at me, she wants a boy. I think she hopes she can raise a son to replace me. If she's not mad at me, she seems to want a girl, and she acts like she's agreeable to using your baby furniture. But you should see what color she wants the nursery painted."

"What is it?"

"Psychedelic green."

"What?"

"Or maybe it's chartreuse, I'm not sure, but she painted

a sample on the wall, and I think it's atrocious. Not that my opinion is worth much around here. But even Celeste's mom thought it was odd. She called it acid green."

"*Acid* green?"

"Of course, Celeste calls it *apple* green, but I call it sickening—it makes my teeth hurt."

Anna laughed. "It sounds, uh, very interesting."

"Honestly, Anna, our baby's vision could be at serious risk if Celeste gets her way on this one."

"Well, maybe she'll change her mind."

"That's possible. But at this rate, she might go for something like fire-hydrant yellow or traffic-cone orange."

"Maybe she should wait to see whether it's a girl or boy to make up her mind."

"That's exactly what I told her."

❦

Later that day, as Anna and Meredith met at their friend Nicole's house to put together their picnic baskets, Anna relayed the story of the "acid green" baby nursery.

"You gotta be kidding," Nicole said as she bent down to wipe the nose of one of her fifteen-month-old twins. Anna wasn't sure if it was Evan or Derrick, but she wondered if they'd get much done with three toddler boys clambering about in the family room. So far it seemed that Nicole and Meri were spending more time refereeing their boys than assembling the baskets. As a result, Anna was trying to work twice as fast.

"I think Celeste should try getting up in the middle of the night and, while she's still half asleep, turn on the light in the nursery. Then see what she thinks about that color," Meredith suggested. "The world looks a lot different at three in the morning."

"Poor David said it actually made his teeth hurt," Anna said.

Meri laughed. "I can just imagine it."

"Here's another thought," Nicole said. "When Celeste gets up at three a.m., David should pop in a soundtrack of a screaming baby—then ask her how she likes that color."

Meri nodded. "And I have just the baby to make a recording."

"You guys should tell David about our little plan," Nicole said.

"I think I will," Meri said. "I mean, just one sleep-deprived night and a simulated screaming baby, and I'll bet Celeste decides that she hates that bright color."

"But I thought you preferred bright colors for babies, Meri." Anna rolled up a yellow-checked tablecloth and inserted it into a basket, nestling it next to the matching yellow plates.

"If you've noticed, I don't have bright colors on my nursery walls," she pointed out. "For my peace and for sanity's sake, I picked out a nice sky blue shade. But, for the sake of Jackson's brain development, everything else in there is pretty bright and colorful."

"But you said he's crying a lot at night?" Anna asked.

"I think he's teething." Meredith sighed. "Just when I thought he was beginning to sleep through the night too. It's like they say . . . a mother's job is never done."

"Tell me about it," Nicole said. "When Kent heard we were having twins, he acted so supportive, like he was so into this. He told me over and over how he was going to help out with everything—how he couldn't wait to be a daddy."

"But he's not doing that now?" Anna glanced at Nicole in time to see her roll her eyes.

"Yeah, right." She tore open the plastic on a package of plates. "I keep telling him that as soon as the boys are potty trained and a little older, he's going to be taking them with him everywhere he goes on the weekends. I don't care whether it's fishing or a ball game or going to Home Depot or whatever—boys need their daddy time, and trust me, they're going to get it." She sighed. "And me . . . well, I'll just be relaxing in a bubble bath or reading a good book or getting a pedicure or eating chocolates . . . or all of the above."

"Sounds like a good plan to me," Meredith said. "Mind if I send Todd and Jackson along with them? I could use a little downtime myself."

"Yeah, we'll send them on boy trips," Nicole continued. "Like camping for the whole weekend."

"Better make sure they can swim first." Meredith set a finished basket off to one side. "The way Todd keeps an eye on Jackson is frightening."

"I know what you mean," Nicole said.

"I asked Todd to watch Jackson while I fixed dinner last night—you know, a home-cooked meal for a change—and after a while I noticed it was really quiet in there. So I look out, and Todd's sitting on the couch, reading the paper, and Jackson is sitting on the floor with a piece of newspaper shoved into his mouth, like he's eating it. At first I think it's kind of funny, but then I realize that Jackson has shoved so much newspaper into his mouth that he's literally gagging. So I run over and stick in my finger and pull out this huge, gray gob of wet newspaper that's nearly suffocating my baby, and Todd doesn't even look up from his paper."

"You're kidding," Anna said. "Was Jackson okay?"

"Well, as soon as I got the gunk out of his mouth he started crying really loud, and I think he was scared. But other than ink stains all over his face, hands, and tongue, he was okay. Although it may set back his reading skills."

"What'd Todd say?" Nicole asked. "Was he sorry?"

"He acted like it was no big deal, like Jackson was fine—end of story."

"So typical."

"Surely Todd felt bad," Anna said. But the glances the moms both gave her looked skeptical. So Anna got quiet. And she just packed baskets and listened as her sister and friend went on with more horror stories of daddy neglect and how men were basically useless when it came to babies. These were occasionally interrupted by settling squabbles between the three toddlers.

Anna didn't comment on their stories, but she felt certain that Michael would've been different as a dad. If only they'd had the chance. She'd always imagined Michael taking an active role with their baby. Of course, she had nothing to base this assumption on. And, to be fair, she was feeling a bit neglected herself these days—what with him putting in so many hours on the new business. How much worse would she feel if she were stuck home with a baby and no help? But, no, she knew that would be different. For starters, she would be so thankful for a baby that she felt certain she would rarely complain, if ever. And, although she would never mention it, she secretly resented the way Meri and Nicole took their gifts of motherhood so lightly. What if the tables were turned?

"Oh man, do you remember how it felt to sleep in on weekends?" Nicole said. "You'd see the sun coming in the window and just roll over and snooze."

"Now I can hardly remember what it felt like to sleep uninterrupted through a whole night."

"Or how about how it felt to take a nice long shower or use the bathroom without little fists pounding on the door, saying 'let me in!'?"

"Are you kidding?" Meredith said. "I don't even bother to

close the bathroom door anymore—the second I do, Jackson starts howling like I've abandoned him."

Nicole laughed. "Speaking of closed doors . . . what about when you want a private moment with your man—it's like the twins have this special radar, like they have some sixth sense that I've slipped into a sexy nightie and dabbed on some perfume—and suddenly they're dying of thirst and they both desperately need a 'dink a wata.'"

"Well, that's not a problem in our house," Meredith said in an uptight voice. "I told Todd that he's not getting any until I start getting a full night of sleep."

"Seriously?" Nicole looked concerned. "That can't be good for your marriage."

Meri just shrugged. "It is what it is."

Nicole pointed at Anna. "You're the lucky one, you know. You and Michael totally have it made."

Anna didn't know how to respond to this. So she didn't. She just kept focused on filling the basket in front of her.

"Not having kids can be very rewarding," Nicole continued blithely. "Do you know how good you have it, Anna?"

"Oh, I wouldn't say that," Meredith said quickly, her eyes flashing a warning at their friend. Anna knew that Meri was fully aware that this was still a sore spot with her. For that matter, so was Nicole.

"There are lots of times when I'd gladly trade places with you, Anna." Nicole sighed loudly as she adjusted the bow on the basket. "Seriously, you are so lucky to be able to call your life your own."

"Yes," Anna said slowly, trying to prevent the bitterness from overcoming her, although she knew that it was useless. There was no way she could ignore Nicole's insensitivity any longer. "I am so lucky . . . like when I went by myself to get a Christmas tree last weekend, I so enjoyed watching other parents with their children while I so conveniently had none. And I'm so lucky to have an empty nursery with expensive baby furniture that my sister-in-law, who doesn't even want to be pregnant, feels isn't good enough for her baby. And I'm so lucky that Michael and I are still in debt over all the painful, and did I mention humiliating, treatments that we endured all for noth—"

"Oh, Anna," Nicole said quickly. "I'm sorry. I didn't mean to say that. Really, I didn't. I was just getting carried away with my stupid little mommy pity party. Please, forgive me!"

But Anna was crying now, and Nicole's apology only made her feel worse. Why hadn't Anna just kept her mouth shut—allowed this to pass like she usually did? Tears only made it worse.

"Please, don't be upset," Meredith said with worried eyes. "We're obviously just a couple of morons, Anna. Please forgive us."

"That's right," Nicole agreed. "We're just a couple of selfish mommy morons."

"We weren't thinking clearly," Meri continued. "I mean, here I am totally sleep deprived, and Nicole's bickering twins could drive anyone nuts—surely you can understand that we're not at our best just now."

"It's okay," Anna said, standing and wishing for a tissue to blot her tears. "I think I'm just, you know, hormonal or something." She wished she could stop crying, but it only seemed to be getting worse. And she was embarrassed to be reacting like this. She usually took this kind of thing in stride, at least on the outside.

"I'm sorry, you guys . . ." Anna grabbed her coat and her purse. "I hate to bail on you, but do you mind if I leave a little early?" She looked at the line of finished baskets. "It looks like we're almost done anyway."

"Please, don't go because of what I said," Nicole persisted. "I'm just—" But her words were cut short by a fight between her twins, and it looked like one of them was in serious peril of being clobbered with a red plastic baseball bat.

"Go ahead and take off, Anna." Meri waved dismissively. "We can easily finish the rest of these." She shook her head. "But really, I am sorry."

"It's okay," Anna said again. "I'm probably just overreacting."

"Drive carefully, sis," Meri called as Anna made her way toward the door.

Nicole paused from where she was still attempting to disengage her boys and made a feeble wave. "See you on Sunday, Anna."

"The baskets really look good," Anna called as she blinked back more hot tears. "We should make a lot of money at the bazaar." Then she was outside, the cool air chilling her still-wet cheeks. She quietly closed Nicole's front door, shutting out the noise of the three toddlers and their disenchanted mothers, and hurried to her car. But once inside, she just sat there, continuing to cry. She knew that this was about more than simply being childless. More than ever, she was feeling like such an outsider. It was as if her illness was building a wall around her, isolating her from people she loved—people who loved her. And yet, she saw no other way to handle it. At least not until after the New Year.

Besides, she thought as she started the car, it was wrong for her sister and friend to joke like that in front of her. It was selfish to complain and commiserate over something that Anna could never hope to fully understand, something she would never be able to relate to. Sure, maybe they were tired of being mommies, but even so.

To be fair, Anna suspected that if she and Michael had

been able to have children, she might've acted similar to her sister and friend. Maybe she would've grumbled about those very same problems—sleepless nights, fussy teething babies, or a husband who was less than helpful. Anna was no saint, and she would've likely participated in her share of whining. If nothing else, she would've indulged in their complaint department simply to fit in.

But underneath it all, Anna felt certain that she'd still be very, very thankful for motherhood. And, she told herself as she pulled into her driveway, Nicole and Meredith were probably thankful too—at least on a good day. She felt certain that, despite their frivolous words, they wouldn't exchange being moms for anything—not a lifetime supply of chocolate, massages, bubble baths, pedicures, or anything.

10

"Beth," Anna said with surprise as she returned to her classroom, "you're still here?"

The little girl nodded from where she was sitting quietly at her desk with her jacket on and her hands folded in front of her. But it was nearly four o'clock and the classroom had long since been vacated. "My grandma was supposed to pick me up," she said. "But I think she forgot." Beth had only been in Anna's class for a few weeks now. There had been some undisclosed problem with her parents, and now, as Anna understood it, her paternal grandmother was taking care of her.

"Do you want me to call her for you?"

"The office lady tried already."

"She's not home?"

Beth shook her head, looking up with sad blue eyes. "Is it okay for me to stay here, Mrs. Jacobs?"

"Of course," Anna said. "Maybe you'd like to help me."

Beth brightened. "Sure. I love helping. What do you want me to do?"

Now Anna had to think quickly. "Well, it's Friday," she said.

"That means the goldfish must be fed for the weekend. And you could check the water of the Christmas tree . . . we want to be sure that it doesn't dry up before Monday."

"Okay," Beth said.

Anna thought of a few more tasks, and Beth turned out to be a good helper, but the clock was still ticking and Anna wasn't sure what she should do about this seemingly forgotten child. "Does your grandmother have a cell phone?" Anna asked.

"Yes. But I can't remember the number."

"Oh." Anna frowned. "How about other relatives? Aunts or uncles?"

"No . . ."

"How about your parents?" Now Anna suspected this wasn't an option, but she was curious about Beth's circumstances.

Beth just looked down at her feet and shrugged.

"Hmm . . ." Anna was ready to go home, but she couldn't just abandon her student. "And Mrs. Scott tried all the numbers in your records."

"It's just my grandma's phone number."

"You don't have an emergency number?"

"I don't know."

"Maybe we should check." So Anna gathered up her things and Beth got her backpack, and they went to the office to discover that no one was there. In fact, it seemed that everyone except the janitor was gone now. Not that it was so unusual for this time of day, or for a Friday.

Anna knelt down to look at Beth. "Well, what do you think we should do?"

Beth shrugged and played with the zipper on her puffy pink jacket. "I dunno."

"I could take you with me, and we could try to reach your grandmother."

82

"Okay." Beth looked up and smiled.

Still, Anna was unsure. In her eight years of teaching, she'd never taken a student home with her before, and she certainly didn't want to be accused of kidnapping. "Let's try your grandmother's phone one more time first," she said after they got into the car. Beth recited the number, and Anna used her cell phone to call. When she got an answering machine, she left a very clear and concise message, informing the woman of what she was doing and giving her phone numbers as well as her address.

"Okay," Anna said. "That should do it."

"Do you have kids?" Beth asked as Anna started her car.

"No. But I do have a dog."

"What's your dog's name?"

"Huntley. And he happens to like kids."

"I like dogs too."

"Do you have a dog?"

"I used to have a dog . . . back before . . ."

"And your grandma doesn't have a dog?"

"No. She's allergic."

"Oh . . ."

"Do you know about my parents?" Beth asked suddenly.

"No . . . not really." Anna wasn't sure whether she should encourage Beth to talk about it or not. For some reason Anna suspected it wasn't a happy story.

"I can tell you," Beth said.

"If you want . . ."

"My grandma doesn't like to talk about it," Beth said. "But I go to see a counselor. Her name is Julie, and she says it's good for me to talk about it."

"Julie sounds like a smart woman."

"She is. I see her on Wednesdays, after school."

"That's good."

"My mommy killed my dad."

Anna felt a cold jolt going through her, but she didn't want Beth to notice. "Really?" she said evenly.

"I wasn't there when she did it . . . I was at school."

"Oh . . ." Anna sneaked a peek at the calm little girl sitting next to her.

"My dad was mean to Mommy. I think that's why she did it."

"Uh-huh." Anna swallowed hard.

"But Mommy is in prison now."

"That must be hard."

"Yeah. I miss her."

"Do you write letters to her?"

"Yeah. Julie helps me with that. Grandma doesn't want to talk to my mommy."

"Your grandma is probably very sad about what happened."

"She is."

"I'm sure you must be very sad too."

"Yeah. At first I cried a lot."

Anna nodded. "I think it's good to cry sometimes." Then Anna told Beth a little about her own mom. "I was really sad when she died, but sometimes my dad didn't want me to cry."

"Like my grandma?"

"Maybe so. But now I think that it's good to cry when you're sad. I think God made us this way for a reason."

"Maybe it's because he knew we needed to get cleaned out," Beth said.

"Yes," Anna agreed as she parked in her driveway. "I think you're right."

"Is this your house?"

"It is." Anna was glad she'd gotten that timer for the lights now.

"I like it," Beth said. "And I like your Christmas lights."

"Wait until you see the tree," Anna said.

Beth had barely had time to see the tree and meet Huntley before her grandmother called. "I am so sorry," she told Anna. "I completely forgot that I was going to pick up Beth. I left work early to go to a dentist appointment and then got distracted and totally forgot to pick her up. I thought she'd ride the school bus like usual. Then I get home and find all these messages. I just feel so terrible."

"It's okay," Anna assured her. She patted Beth's head as she spoke. "Beth is a delight to have around, and I've enjoyed her company."

"Well, I'm on my way to your house right now," Mrs. Albert said. "I so appreciate you looking out for her like this. You know, this being a parent again is taking some getting used to."

"I'll bet."

"And I'm a single woman," she continued. "It's just little Beth and me now."

"Well, she's a great kid," Anna said. "You're blessed to have her."

"Yes . . . that's true."

They said good-bye and Anna hung up. "Your grandmother is on her way," she told Beth. "And she feels terrible for forgetting about you."

"It's okay," said Beth as she petted Huntley. "It was fun coming to your house, and I like your dog."

Anna was just about to offer Beth a snack when she heard the doorbell ring. "I'll bet that's your grandmother now."

And it was, but Anna was surprised that this "grandma" didn't look too much older than herself. Also, she had on a short skirt and knee-high boots. Not your typical grandma type.

"I am so sorry," Mrs. Albert repeated. She knelt down and hugged Beth. "You must think that your grandmother is a complete nincompoop."

Beth laughed. "No. You just forgot, Grandma. It's okay. Mrs. Jacobs took really good care of me."

"I enjoyed her company," Anna said.

"Mrs. Jacobs doesn't have kids," Beth informed her grandma. "But she has a really cool dog."

Anna smiled.

"Well, thanks again," Mrs. Albert said. "Have a good weekend."

"Don't forget about the school Christmas concert tomorrow," Anna reminded her.

"Oh, yes." Mrs. Albert actually slapped her forehead. "I have the flyer on the refrigerator, but after today, well, who knows?"

"Well, I'll bet you won't forget, will you, Beth?" Anna asked.

"No way!" Beth grinned. "See ya tomorrow, Mrs. Jacobs." Then she and her grandma trotted off toward what looked like a fairly new Mustang convertible. It seemed that Beth's grandma was setting a new youthful standard for grandparents.

Anna closed the front door and went back to the kitchen, where Huntley looked up at her expectantly, like he wanted to know what had become of his young playmate.

"I suppose you miss Beth now," she said. His tail thumped back and forth as if to confirm this. "Well, sorry, old boy, but we can't keep her."

Yet even as Anna said this, a lump formed in her throat. Of course she hadn't expected to keep her student. But why was it that now her house felt much emptier than usual? And why was it that some people were "blessed" with children that they didn't really want or couldn't take care of? The idea of Beth's mother killing her father and now doing time in prison actually made Anna's head hurt. She didn't want to judge them, but what about poor Beth—why should she suddenly be parentless and be raised by a grandma who forgot to pick her up from school? What else might she forget? And what about people like Anna and Michael who wanted desperately to be parents but were forced to be childless? What was fair about that?

These were not new questions. But they were some of the things she intended to ask God about someday. Maybe someday in the not too distant future too. But Anna didn't really want to think about that right now—she wanted to pretend like she didn't know what was going on or that her stomach hadn't bothered her a lot today. Denial seemed to be her only protection for the time being, and she planned to wear it like a warm winter coat until January. She turned on the teakettle, but even green tea didn't sound very appetizing. Maybe some saltines would be better. She wondered how advanced this thing really was—how long it had been since she'd experienced the first symptoms. Or what kind of prognosis she was risking by delaying treatment. Not that it had made any difference with her mother. Why would it with her?

Again, she told herself not to think about such things. Focus on Christmas instead—make memories and happy times. Celebrate each day fully. But even as she tried to do this, she could feel those all-too-familiar tears filling her eyes once again. Anna reached for a tissue, and as she blew her nose, she reminded herself of what Beth had said—how crying cleaned them out. Anna thought she should be pretty clean by now.

Somehow Anna made it through the weekend's blur of activities and commitments without having any more emotional breakdowns. Perhaps being busy was the best defense against the blues. Oh, sure, she'd been somewhat overcome while watching her class of second graders performing their rendition of "Little Drummer Boy" for the Christmas concert—for which Beth was on time and was wearing an adorable red velvet dress. But then, Anna always got a little weepy at that particular event. And she'd been so happy that all their baskets sold at the bazaar—bringing in more than $500 for the Darfur fund—that she'd been a little teary-eyed for that too. But then so had Nicole and Meredith. Or maybe they were still feeling bad about the other night.

But by Monday, after all the busyness of the weekend, Anna realized that she really hadn't had much quality time with Michael. And this was driven home further when he announced that, once again, he would be working late tonight.

"I miss you," she complained as he filled his travel mug with coffee.

"I miss you too," he said. "But trust me, this overtime thing is not going to last forever."

"Maybe 'forever' is in the eyes of the beholder," she told him.

He laughed, then leaned down to peck her on the cheek. Still, she hadn't meant to be funny. More and more she was realizing that time—each precious, one-of-a-kind day—was not a renewable resource.

11

"Anna, this is Meri. It's Wednesday, around two o'clock, and I really, really need to talk to you. As soon as possible. Please, call me when you get this message. Really, it's urgent." Anna replayed the message just to make sure she'd heard it right, then hit the speed dial for Meri's cell phone.

"What's wrong?" she asked her sister as soon as she answered.

"Thanks for calling," Meri said in a voice that sounded much calmer than the message she'd left. "Where are you right now?"

"In the school parking lot." Anna unlocked her car. "Just getting into my car. But tell me, Meri, is something really wrong? Is it Dad? Or David? Or—"

"No. Dad and David are fine. Well, as far as I know. But this isn't about them."

"What then?"

"It's about me. Can you meet me at Starbucks on Fifth Street?"

"Sure."

"Okay, I'm on my way."

Anna's heart was still pounding hard as she started her car. What was wrong with Meri? Was it possible that she, like Anna, was experiencing the symptoms for ovarian cancer? What if they both were sick? How devastating would that be for the rest of the family?

"Please, God," Anna pleaded as she turned onto Fifth Street. "Please, don't let Meri be sick too. That would be too much. Please, let her be fine. Please!"

Anna parked in front, then jumped out of her car just as Meri pulled up. Anna ran over and hugged her. "Are you okay?" she demanded, stepping back to look right into her sister's eyes.

"That depends . . ." Meri glanced away. "Come on, let's go inside. I'll explain."

Anna's stomach had been worse than usual again today, so she simply got a bottle of water, then went over to a quiet table and waited for Meri to join her with her latte.

"Please, tell me what's wrong," Anna said after Meri sat down. "I can't take the suspense. Is it your health?"

"No. Well, not my physical health anyway. Some people, Todd in particular, might question the state of my mental health, though."

Anna stared at her sister with impatience. "Explain."

"I think I want a divorce."

Anna blinked. "A divorce?"

Meredith nodded, then looked down at her latte.

"Are you serious?" Anna wanted to grab Meri by her shoulders and violently shake her. She wanted to say things like, "Are you crazy?" or "Have you lost your mind?" or "Have you forgotten that you and Todd have a child?"

Meredith looked back up at her. "I am serious."

Anna sucked in a quick breath. "Why?"

"It's a long story . . ."

"I have lots of time." Okay, maybe that was an overstatement.

"And Jackson still has an hour left at the babysitter's."

That was another thing that Anna silently disapproved of. Meredith had gone back to work after only six weeks of maternity leave. Todd had encouraged her to stay home for the first year, pointing out that they would spend nearly half her salary on child care, but Meredith had insisted. And Anna still didn't get it.

"Okay, Meri," Anna said, trying to sound a lot more understanding than she felt just now. "Tell me what's going on with you and Todd."

"Remember how I felt we were drifting apart before I got pregnant?"

Anna nodded. "Yes. But then it seemed like things changed."

"Things did change. But not between Todd and me. I was so obsessed with having the baby, I thought it was going to magically fix everything. But I was wrong."

"It seems unfair to expect a baby to fix everything, Meri."

"Yes, I know." She sighed. "But I thought maybe it would make Todd and me closer. I thought it would ignite that old spark."

"From what I've heard, it's usually just the opposite, isn't it? I mean, the way you and Nicole were going on about it . . . well, it didn't sound too good."

"Yeah, well, at least Nicole and Kent still love each other."

"Meaning?"

"Meaning I don't love Todd. And, despite the fact that he doesn't want a divorce, I don't think he loves me either." Her eyes glistened with tears.

Anna reached across the table and took her sister's hand. "Oh, Meri . . ."

"I wish it was different, Anna. Really, I do. But how can I be expected to stay in a marriage without love?"

"Maybe it's just a stage."

"That's what I used to tell myself too."

"Maybe when Jackson is a little older . . . a little more independent . . . maybe things will get better."

Meri just shook her head. "I don't think so."

"How can you be so sure?"

"I just know."

"I don't see how you can know that, Meri. I mean, Michael and I have had some rough times too. And that didn't involve children . . . well, not exactly anyway. But we weathered those times. And we love each other more than ever now."

Meri looked at Anna with hopeful eyes. "Yes. And that's what I want too."

"But you have to work at it, Meri. That's what I'm saying. You can't just throw in the towel."

"Sometimes you have to."

"But why? And what about your vows? You guys are Christians too. You're supposed to take this kind of thing seriously."

"I do take it seriously."

"Then how can you give up?"

Meredith looked down at her latte again, and something in her expression—perhaps that quick sideways glance—reminded Anna of when they were teenagers. It was the same look that Meri had gotten when she'd done something wrong—something that Anna had to try to cover up for her. Anna let go of her sister's hand and sat up straighter.

"What's really going on?" Anna asked.

"What do you mean?"

"You know what I mean, Meri. What's really going on here?"

Meredith pressed her lips together, then looked around, as if to see if anyone was near enough to hear her. "I'm in love with someone else."

Anna felt dizzy. She took in a deep breath to steady herself, wondering if this was another symptom of her illness or just an emotional reaction to Meri's confession.

"I know, I know . . ." Meri shook her head. "It's wrong. And I'm not proud of it. But it's the truth. And I just really needed to talk to someone—besides Todd, that is."

"Todd knows?"

"Not really, but he might suspect something." Meri looked down again.

"Have you—have you been having an affair?"

Meredith looked up with an offended expression. "No, of course not."

Anna held up her hands. "Hey, I don't know. You have to admit, this is pretty shocking news, Meri."

"Like I said, I'm not proud of myself."

"Who is the guy?"

"He's a social worker too. His name is Cooper, and he's— well, he's everything that Todd is not."

"Is he married?"

"Divorced."

"Oh . . ." Anna really didn't know how to react to any of this. She couldn't have been more surprised if Meredith had announced she'd just booked a trip to Mars on the next space shuttle. How had this happened? Why hadn't Anna known?

"I know you're shocked, Anna. But really, who else could I talk to?"

"It's a lot to take in . . . I mean, I never would've guessed this in a thousand years, Meri. So, how long have you been, you know, in love with this Cooper dude?" Even saying that name felt foreign to Anna—like something acidic on her tongue. She had never met the guy, and she felt like she hated him already. And Anna didn't hate anyone.

"I've always admired him. He's so great with people, and he loves kids."

"Does he *have* kids?"

"A five-year-old daughter."

"But he's divorced."

"Yes."

"How long?"

"Not quite a year."

"Does he have custody?"

"They share it."

"Oh . . ." Anna wanted to point out how complicated Meredith's life would become. She'd seen these situations at school. Stepparents, stepchildren, stepsiblings . . . everyone trying to figure out where they fit in, trying to remember whose turn it was to have the kids. Kind of like Beth's situation, only with more people involved.

"And Cooper really loves Jackson," Meri said.

"He's met him?"

"Well, yeah . . ."

Anna wanted to ask how but didn't. "How does Cooper feel about you?"

"The same."

"But you really haven't slept with him?"

"No." Meredith firmly shook her head. "I wouldn't do that, Anna. I'm not like that."

Anna wanted to scream, "You're not like this either!" But it seemed pointless. Instead she said, "So, what am I supposed to say?"

"I don't know . . ."

"You must know that I'm not supportive of this. You must know that all I can do is recommend that you work things out with Todd. Have you considered seeing a marriage counselor?"

"I asked Todd to go with me more than a year ago, but he refused. He thought it was a waste of time and money."

"What about now?" Anna asked.

"Now it's too late."

"Really?" Anna peered curiously at her sister, trying to determine who this person was—and had she always been this way? Or had something changed? Was it partially Anna's fault for not paying closer attention? In some ways, Anna had taken a parental role in her younger sister's life, although they were only two and a half years apart. She'd helped her in school, with relationships, with planning her wedding; she'd even been Meri's birthing coach when Jackson was born. What more could she have done? Paid closer attention, perhaps.

"I knew you would take this hard," Meredith said. "But I also knew that I needed to talk to someone—I felt like I was about to explode."

"And you can," Anna said. "Talk to me, I mean. It's just that I can't see how getting a divorce will be the best thing for you. A marriage is a lifetime commitment, something you have to work at, invest yourself into, and when it's hard, you simply try harder . . . and eventually it smoothes out, your efforts pay off."

"Maybe for you."

Anna bit her lip.

"I'm sorry to disappoint you."

"What about Todd?"

"I feel bad about Todd. But I do not see how staying with

him will help anything. We're both miserable, Anna. Staying together won't improve that."

"What about Jackson?"

"Same thing. Staying in a lousy marriage isn't good for children."

"Will you marry Cooper?"

"I don't know . . . maybe . . ."

"But he's been divorced, Meri. Don't you see a pattern here?"

"His wife had an affair."

"Oh . . ."

"You'd like him, Anna. I know you would."

Anna felt certain that Meri was wrong.

"He's very sweet and genuine. And if you met him, you'd be shocked that I love him. I mean, he's not even handsome."

Anna blinked. This was surprising. Meredith had always been attracted to the tall, dark, and handsome types. Like Todd. "You're saying that he's not attractive?"

"He's attractive to me, Anna. But he's not what you'd call handsome. He's actually sort of geeky looking."

"Geeky?"

"Yeah. He's starting to bald and he's pretty skinny and he's about the same height as me, so I can't wear heels when I'm with him."

Anna shook her head. This was just too weird. Her sister sitting here in Starbucks talking about what kind of footwear she could sport with her new boyfriend. "So . . . what happens next?" Anna asked.

"For starters, you can't tell a soul."

"Why?"

"I don't want to ruin Christmas."

"Right." Anna shook her head.

"I know, it sounds dumb. But it's Jackson's first Christmas, and I just wanted to get through it, you know? Dad and Donna are having us all over for Christmas Eve . . . and David and Celeste are expecting. And I just want everyone to be happy, you know. I don't want to rock the boat."

"So, what then? The day after Christmas . . . you sink the boat?"

"I'll wait a week or so."

"Right . . ."

"You think I should tell everyone now?"

Anna considered this. She also considered the secret she was keeping from her family until after Christmas—or New Year's. Perhaps between her and Meredith, they would simply cancel out the shock for one another.

"You know I love you, Meredith," Anna said finally. "And no matter what you do, I'll always love you. But I really want what's best for you."

Meredith smiled. "Then you should be happy for me."

Anna closed her eyes and took a deep breath. She felt sick again and dizzy still. She slowly opened her eyes and took a sip of water.

"Are you okay?"

"Just a stomach thing," she admitted. "Leftover flu bug."

Meredith studied her closely. "I thought that stomach flu was months ago."

"Maybe this is a new one." She forced a smile. "One of the fringe benefits of working with kids, you know."

"At least you only have two more days before Christmas break. That's got to feel good."

"Yes. I can't wait. Hey, you haven't been over to see my Christmas tree yet."

"How about if I bring Jackson by on Saturday?"

"Great."

"I want Christmas to be perfect for him. I know some

people don't believe that babies can remember things at this age, but I feel certain they can. And I want Jackson's first Christmas to be happy and unspoiled."

Anna wanted to ask about the following Christmases. What about sharing custody? Who got Thanksgiving? Who got Easter? Surely Meredith had to realize that those holidays might not all be "happy and unspoiled." But mostly Anna felt tired. All she wanted to do was go home and go to bed. Meredith was right about one thing today: Anna was counting the hours until Christmas break. She was ready for a rest.

12

"You're working late again?" Anna said.

"I'm sorry, sweetie," Michael told her. "Can't be avoided."

"But it's Friday night and Christmas break has officially begun. I wanted to celebrate!"

"Can we celebrate tomorrow?"

"I don't know." She felt like pouting. "For all I know, you'll decide to work again."

"I won't. I promise. Tomorrow night I'll be home and we'll do something special. Okay?"

"Okay."

"And if it makes you feel any better, you know that I'd much rather be home with you than working, don't you?"

"Yeah, I guess so . . ."

"Come on, Anna. You know that's the truth."

"Yes, I know. And I do appreciate how hard you're working to make your business a success, Michael. Sorry to sound so grumpy. It's just that I miss you."

"I miss you too."

"And I was going to make lasagna for dinner tonight."

"Oh, now you're really making me feel bad."

"Good."

He laughed. "Well, just enjoy your leisure, little lady. Three and a half weeks to do whatever you please. I'm starting to feel jealous."

"Why don't you take some time off too?" she said suddenly. "Maybe we could go do something—take a trip or something?"

"It sounds great, honey. But you know how finances are just now."

"Oh, yeah . . ."

"Maybe next year, when we're all caught up."

"Yeah, sure . . . next year."

Anna tried not to feel sorry for herself when she hung up the phone. Then, as she was putting away the lasagna ingredients, she thought about poor Michael, slaving away at the office, probably sending for takeout again. Well, that settled it. She'd just go ahead and make the lasagna tonight after all. If she jumped right on it, she could have it delivered to Michael and his partner Grant in time for dinner.

⁂

She could hear the hot lasagna still bubbling beneath the foil as she slipped it into the cardboard box that she'd lined with kitchen towels. She'd already put a green salad, a loaf of French bread, and some plates and silverware in the car. She couldn't wait to see the expressions on Michael's and Grant's faces when they saw their feast.

She'd meant to call them but had gotten so busy that she'd forgotten. But they didn't usually order out until around 6:30 anyway, so she thought she was safe. But when she got to the office, it looked like the lights were off inside. Still, she carried the box containing the lasagna up the stairs and knocked on the door. No answer. Had they gone out for dinner? Was she too late?

"Hey," a male voice called from the bottom of the stairs. "Is that you, Anna?"

"Grant?"

She could hear him clomping up the stairs now. "What are you doing here?"

She held out the box. "Dinner."

"Wow, that smells amazing. But why did you bring it here?"

"Aren't you guys working late tonight?"

"I'm not. Suzy and I have a Christmas party to go to."

"Oh . . ." She frowned.

"But maybe Michael planned to work tonight." Yet, even as Grant said this, she detected a question mark in his voice. As if he wasn't too sure but thought maybe he was covering for his partner, which she found irksome.

"Well, maybe I got my wires crossed," she said. "I thought he was working tonight."

"Maybe he's at home by now," Grant said. "Wondering what happened to dinner."

"Maybe so," Anna said. And maybe Grant was right. Perhaps her lonely plea had gotten to Michael and, realizing that Grant was going to a Christmas party, Michael had changed his mind and gone home. For all she knew they might've passed each other in traffic just now—like the old proverbial ships in the night. "I better go," she said quickly. "Before the lasagna gets cold."

"Lasagna?" He smacked his lips loudly. "Now I actually wish Michael and I *were* working late tonight. I haven't had a good lasagna in ages."

"Maybe next time," she called out as she headed back down the stairs.

But when she got home, Michael wasn't there. And, as far as she could tell, he hadn't been there either. She set the lasagna box on the counter and frowned down at Huntley. "Guess it's just you and me tonight, old boy."

She took her time serving up a plate for herself. She knew it was because she was hoping that Michael was going to pop in and surprise her. Perhaps with flowers or a bottle of wine. He did that sometimes—just for the fun of it. But it had been awhile since he had surprised her like that. And when she finally sat down to eat, it was by herself. And, although she loved lasagna just as much as Michael, it didn't taste quite right to her tonight. She'd only eaten a few bites when her stomach began to feel upset again.

So she focused on the bread and salad instead, but she soon realized it was useless. She had no appetite, just an uneasy feeling deep inside her. She didn't want to think about it, but she couldn't help imagining the insidious mass of cancer cells quietly growing deep within her. She cleared the little dining table, then set up her laptop and before long was surfing the Internet, looking for more information on ovarian cancer. She wanted to find something new and hopeful . . . something encouraging. But mostly it was just the same old story. The same list of symptoms, all the very things she was experiencing. And always, the same old advice to see your doctor as soon as possible. She even searched out some "alternative" sites, but their suggestions sounded a little scary to her. Plus she read from other more reliable sites that alternative medicine for the treatment of ovarian cancer was questionable and highly discouraged. Finally, feeling dejected and even more sick to her stomach, she turned off her computer and went to finish cleaning the kitchen.

But where was Michael? More disturbing than the

question of her health was the question of her husband's whereabouts tonight. And perhaps that was contributing to her stomachache as well. She wanted to call him and ask what was up, but she knew that would sound suspicious. Besides, it was possible he'd run out to grab a bite to eat, then returned to the office. It was possible he was sitting in front of his computer right now, immersed in some important project—and a phone call might interrupt his chain of thought and force him to work even later. No, the bottom line was that she trusted Michael. She knew that in her core. She just wished she knew for certain where he was right now—and if he was okay.

As she turned on the dishwasher, she even considered driving back over there to see if the office lights were on or if his car was parked in its space. Just to make sure he was all right—kind of like a guardian angel. But she was bone tired. Cooking that dinner had sapped what little energy she had . . . and now all she wanted to do was to sleep. She freshened the water in Huntley's bowl and turned off the kitchen lights, then took a comforting shower, using some lovely lavender shower gel that a student's mother had given her for Christmas. And then, though it wasn't even nine yet, she went to bed.

⬥

"You must've been tired last night," Michael told her the next morning as he held out a steaming cup before her. "Care for some coffee in bed?"

She made a face. "No, no thanks. My stomach is a little upset."

"Oh . . ." He blinked and stepped back. "Sorry. I just remembered how you used to like coffee in bed on Saturday mornings."

"Not this morning." She quickly got up and hurried past him toward the bathroom. Was he trying to make up for something with her? Coffee in bed? It had been years since they'd done that. She splashed water on her face. What was he up to anyway? Was he acting guilty? And why was she feeling so suspicious? Was her illness inducing paranoia too? Maybe she should check for those symptoms on the Internet. Or maybe her worries over Michael were related to her sister's confession this week. As she brushed her teeth, she thought about Meredith's marriage situation and this Cooper guy. It still just made her really mad. What was Meri thinking? Perhaps she wasn't thinking. And perhaps Anna was doing some kind of transference thing with poor Michael, suspecting him simply because of Meredith's irresponsible attitude toward marriage.

She continued to hash over these things until she finally decided that she was being unfair to her husband. But by the time she was dressed and ready to face the world, Michael was gone. Fortunately Huntley was gone too, so she figured they were out on a walk together. Good thing too, since poor old Huntley hadn't been walked in days. Anna turned on the flame under the teakettle, reassuring herself that all was well. She was just pouring a bowl of cornflakes, one of the few food items that didn't seem to bother her digestive system, when the phone rang.

"Hey, sis," Meredith said lightly. "When can Jackson and I come by and check out your Christmas tree?"

"Whenever you like." Anna turned off the flame under the teakettle right before it started to whistle.

"Well, I was thinking this morning would be good. That way I can get in some Christmas shopping later while Jackson is still in good spirits. And then he'll need an afternoon nap and I'll need to stop by the dry cleaner and—"

"This morning is fine," Anna said quickly. She could tell by the way Meri was chattering away that she was still uncomfortable about her situation. Overcommunication had always been one of Meredith's favorite smoke screens—her way to obscure what was really going on. Well, whatever. Anna was just as glad to pretend that nothing was going on too.

"Okay," Meredith said. "We're on our way."

⁘

Michael and Huntley had just gotten home from their walk when Meredith and Jackson arrived. And suddenly the house felt overly full and somewhat like a circus. Naturally, all that Jackson wanted to do was to attack their Christmas tree and eat the popcorn strings and pull on Huntley's ears, although the poor dog finally retreated to the sanctuary of the laundry room. Anna had forgotten what a handful her young nephew could be. But at the same time, it was hard to resist those rosy cheeks, curly hair, and sparkling brown eyes. To Jackson, every new thing was a great adventure that he felt compelled to explore.

"I see you have your hands full," Michael said as Anna set some of the more precious glass ornaments on a high shelf. "I'm going to run to the office to check on some things."

She tossed him a questioning look.

"Don't worry, Anna, I haven't forgotten about tonight. I'll be back in time."

After Michael was gone, Meredith gave Anna a dark scowl. "You told him, didn't you?"

"Told him what?" Anna pried Jackson's chubby fingers from their grasp around the pole lamp, then lifted him up so that he could see the top part of the tree.

"You know what."

"About you?" Anna shook her head. "No way. A promise is a promise."

"But he acted strange. Like he wanted to get away from me, Anna. Like he knew something. You told him, didn't you?"

"No, I did not." Anna was trying to distract Jackson with the stuffed bear that she'd set in a child-sized rocker underneath the tree, although he seemed more interested in turning the rocker into an acrobatic prop than cuddling the bear.

"Then why was he acting like that?"

"Honestly, Meri, he doesn't know a thing. If he looked like he was trying to escape anything, it was probably me." But as soon as she said this, she regretted it.

"Escape you? Yeah, right."

Anna swooped up Jackson just before he tipped over the rocker. "You are a handful, little man," she cooed at him. "No wonder your mom is plum worn out sometimes."

"You're telling me," Meri said as she collapsed into the club chair.

"I can't believe you're taking him Christmas shopping with you today," Anna said. "Talk about being a glutton for punishment."

"I couldn't find a sitter." Meredith looked hopefully at her now. "That is, unless Auntie Anna wants to have a little visitor."

Everything in Anna said to say no. Everything except that part of her that loved babies. Still, she rationalized, she wasn't at her best. It might not be in Jackson's best interests to be watched by her. What about her stomach problems, her lack of energy? And what if she needed to use the bathroom suddenly? Plus her house was in no way baby-proof. "I don't know if that's a good idea, Meri . . ."

"Oh, I didn't figure you would want him. Good grief, his

own daddy doesn't even want him. Maybe this is a baby that only a mother can love."

"No, that's not it. I do love him. And I'd love to watch him. But my house isn't really baby-proof, you know? I'd feel terrible if he got hurt."

"How about the nursery? It's safe, isn't it?"

Anna nodded slowly. "Yeah, actually, it is."

"And Celeste hasn't taken the crib yet. Couldn't Jackson have a nap in there?"

"Sure," Anna said suddenly. "Why not?"

Meredith stood up now and hugged her. "You are the best, Anna. I really don't know what I'd do without you."

Anna forced a smile. Unfortunately that was a problem that Meredith would have to figure out on her own . . . someday.

Meredith handed over the diaper bag along with a few directions, then, just like that, she was gone. For the next couple of hours, Anna chased her nephew around the house, trying to prevent him from harm as much as to prevent him from harming something. She tried to put him down for a nap a couple of times, but whenever she placed him in the crib, he began to howl like he was being tortured. She changed his diaper a couple of times, tried to get him to eat some of his baby food, then gave him his bottle. And when it was nearly three and Anna was exhausted and ready to call her sister and let her know that it was time to pick up her little darling, Jackson finally started to look sleepy.

Anna set the empty bottle aside and quietly carried him to the nursery, where she'd already pulled the blinds down and gotten the bed ready. She gently rocked him in her arms, making sure his pacifier was secure, then softly sang a couple of lullabies. It really was amazing how this child, who'd been bouncing off the walls just minutes ago, could suddenly grow limp and relaxed in her arms, like a hyperactive marionette whose strings had been clipped.

She leaned over and kissed his warm, moist forehead and then, for the third time, gently eased him into the crib. She tucked the comforter—the one she'd picked out for their own baby—snugly around him, then slowly stood back up and just watched him. She was literally holding her breath as she waited for his eyes to pop open and for him to start screaming again. But miraculously he did not.

She tiptoed out of the room, leaving the door ajar so she could hear him if he woke. Then, still tiptoeing, she went into the living room and flopped down onto the sofa. Right now all she wanted was a nap as well. But just as she closed her eyes, she heard a noise at the front door.

"Hello?" Meredith called quietly. "I thought Jackson might still be asleep, so I didn't ring the bell. Hope you don't mind I let myself in."

Anna glanced up from the couch. "Not at all. Excuse me for not getting up, but I don't think I'm able."

"Did he wear you out?"

"He's got a lot of energy. And he just went down for his nap."

"You mean just now?"

"Yes. Like about three minutes ago. I tried to put him down a couple of times earlier, but he was not interested."

"Wow, you look wiped out, Anna."

Anna leaned her head back into the couch and sighed. "I am. Toddlers are exhausting."

Meredith laughed as she sat down in the club chair. "You're telling me."

"What took you so long anyway?"

"I'm sorry. But seriously, it was a total zoo out there."

"So, did you find what you were looking for?"

108

"I guess." Meredith gave her a puzzled look now. "Hey, are you feeling okay, Anna?"

"What do you mean?"

Meredith's frown lines deepened. "I mean, you don't look so good—and, come to think of it, you haven't seemed like your old normal self lately. How are you doing?"

Anna sat up now, hoping to look more like her old self—whatever that was. "I'm perfectly fine."

Meredith looked really skeptical now. "No, you're not."

"What do you mean, no I'm not?"

"I mean, I know you, Anna. Something's wrong. I can tell."

Anna felt her eyes getting hot with tears again. She really did want to talk to someone about all that was going on in her life right now. Someone besides God, although she knew that he had been listening, and she knew that she would be lost without that. But this was Meredith . . . what should Anna tell her? Where would she begin? And where would she end? To be fair, her health problem, at this point, was only a suspicion on her part. Okay, it was a very strong suspicion and the symptoms were real, but it could be nothing. And this thing with Michael, well, that was probably nothing too. In fact, it might simply be her imagination.

"I'm fine . . . really." She forced a tired smile for her sister.

"You mentioned your stomach earlier this week, Anna. Is it still bothering you?"

Anna nodded. Perhaps there was no point in keeping this from Meredith. If anyone knew Anna, besides Michael, it was her sister. "Yeah."

"How long has it been bothering you?"

"I'm not sure . . ." Anna glanced at the clock on the mantel, like that was going to help her. "Maybe a month or two."

"And what's going on exactly? Describe how you feel."

So Anna told her about feeling bloated and unable to eat and the other things. "It's probably nothing."

Meredith came over to sit by Anna on the couch and, with a very serious expression, asked, "Have you been to the doctor yet?"

That did it. The tears were coming now, hot and heavy this time, like the floodgates had been knocked open. Meredith put her arms around Anna and pulled her close. "What's going on, Anna? Please, tell me. What's wrong?"

Finally, when Anna recovered enough to speak, and after she'd blown her nose long and hard, she took a long, deep breath. "I think I might have ovarian cancer."

This time it was Meredith who broke down. She was sobbing now, and Anna was the one comforting her. "It's going to be okay, Meri," she said again and again, although she had no idea how it was going to be okay.

"Oh, Anna," Meredith said finally. "Why didn't you tell me?"

"I don't want anyone to know yet."

"Why not?" Meredith picked up a pillow and punched it hard.

"Because . . . it's Christmas, Meri. I don't want to spoil it. Sort of like you and your marriage troubles. My news can wait."

"But you are getting treatments, right?"

Anna explained the insurance dilemma and how she didn't want to get a diagnosis before they had a policy in place. "They would consider it a previous condition."

"Who cares about insurance! We're talking about your health."

"Don't you understand? Without insurance, we could go bankrupt, Michael could lose his business."

"I don't care. You need to get in to see a doctor, Anna. ASAP."

"A couple of weeks won't hurt and I—"

"Baloney, Anna." Meredith stood up now. "I've read up on this thing. Once I hit my midthirties, I started going in for a checkup every six months. You know that we're both subject to it . . . because of Mom. And you, Anna . . ." Meri shook her fist. "Oh, I should've thought of this sooner. I mean, not only do you look like Mom, you even act like her. You probably have identical DNA."

"I'll take that as a compliment."

"And it is . . . except that it places you at higher risk."

"I'm also the same age as she was."

Meredith blinked in surprise. "Really? That doesn't seem possible."

Anna nodded. "I know . . . but it is."

"And being childless, Anna, you know that places you at higher risk too."

"I know . . . I just read up on it recently myself."

"You mean, you weren't aware of this before—you didn't know what the symptoms were, or what the risk is?"

"Not really."

"But you do know now?" Then Meredith began quizzing Anna, naming all the symptoms as if going over a checklist. And each time, Anna nodded.

"I think it's pretty much a textbook case," Anna admitted.

"And you haven't gone to the doctor?"

"I thought it was the flu, Meri. You know we had a bout with it at school in early October—everyone got hit."

"That was months ago!"

"I know. And I finally put two and two together. I know it's not the flu now. Right after Thanksgiving—just two weeks ago—I sat down and figured it out."

"But you didn't see a doctor."

"I will."

"When?"

"I'll make a doctor appointment next week." She didn't add that she'd make it for January and that she'd pretend like she was simply scheduling a routine gynecological checkup.

"Oh, Anna," Meredith said. "I feel so terrible that I burdened you with my marriage problems and here you are dealing with something like this."

"It's okay." Anna forced a smile. "And maybe I'm okay. Maybe I'm just run-down and need to take better care of myself."

"And here I go leaving Jackson for you to care for."

"It was fun. I love him."

"Does Michael know?"

"No one knows, Meri. Except you."

"And you'll call the doctor on Monday?"

"Absolutely." Anna would call her too. The appointment would be scheduled.

"And maybe you're right," Meredith said. "Maybe you are just run-down. But you need to find out. Knowledge is power, Anna. Especially when it comes to something like this."

"I really do think I'm just worn out from school and everything. It's not unusual for this time of year. And I'm so glad to have Christmas break just now. I'm sure I'll be back to my old self in a week or so."

Meredith nodded. "Yes, you're probably right."

"And I can trust you not to tell anyone."

"Of course." She looked up at the clock. "And now I'm going to slip my little sleeping angel out of here so that you can get some much-needed rest."

"Oh, don't wake him."

"It's okay. He'll go to sleep again . . . as soon as we get home.

And that way I can get a few things done too." Meredith hugged Anna. "And everything's going to be okay, isn't it?"

"Definitely. I know that God's in control of this," Anna said, partly to reassure Meri and partly to convince herself. "I really do have a sense of peace about it."

"Good. Just don't forget to call the doctor, okay? First thing on Monday."

Anna nodded. "It's as good as done."

"Because I need you, sis."

"I need you too."

13

Michael made good on his promise to be home on Saturday night and even offered to take her out, but Anna told him she was too tired. She said that watching Jackson had worn her out, which was partially true. So they stayed home, eating leftover lasagna and watching an old movie. Anna had thought perhaps it would turn into a "romantic" evening, but Michael fell asleep in front of the TV, and Anna was so tired that she headed off to bed herself. But as she brushed her teeth, she realized that she'd never asked him about where he had been the previous evening when she'd attempted to deliver dinner. She had repressed her worries and had told herself that there was some logical explanation and that Michael would tell her all about it and they would laugh and that would be the end of it. But it hadn't happened.

As she turned back the comforter, noticing how Michael's side of the bed was empty, her mind began to churn. Where *had* he been? And what if something was wrong? Seriously wrong? What if he had fallen out of love with her? What if he was involved with someone else? What if he was cheating on her? The mere idea sliced through her like a jagged knife. She could endure a horrible terminal illness, even undergo painful and debilitating treatments for it, but she knew that losing Michael would hurt more than anything else could. In fact, she felt it would kill her. She fluffed the pillow and sighed. She was letting her mind run away with her. Surely Michael was not having an affair. She knew he loved her. She knew their love was the kind of love that only grew stronger over the years. And yet . . . how many other women had thought the same thing, only to be devastated when they learned the truth?

Finally, as she climbed into bed, she told herself she was being completely ridiculous. As Grandma Lily liked to say, she was making a mountain out of a molehill. She decided to simply push it from her mind. *Don't worry*, she reminded herself, *just pray*. And so, before she slipped off to sleep, she did pray.

◦⬦◦

Sunday passed uneventfully, and by the time they went to bed, Anna told herself that everything was just fine between them. Her suspicions about Michael—not that she called them that—were totally ungrounded. As always they were in love. And Anna couldn't wait to see his reaction when she presented his fabulous Christmas present this year. She was hoping and praying that the engine would arrive early and that David would help her to get the car to the mechanics and then parked in the driveway on Christmas morning. With a big red bow. It would be perfect.

The next day Anna called the doctor, scheduling a routine exam. "How about January 16?" the receptionist suggested.

"You don't have anything sooner?"

"Not unless it's urgent."

"The sixteenth is fine." Anna wrote it down, thanked her, and hung up. Hopefully Meredith would be so consumed with her own life and problems that she would forget to ask Anna about her appointment. Anna's plan now was to wait until the week after Christmas before she told Michael that they would need to get some health insurance in place. That was less than two weeks away. And she figured it would look better if they had the insurance for a few weeks before her doctor delivered the diagnosis. So perhaps the sixteenth was for the best anyway.

In the meantime, Anna planned to make the most of Christmas. She had shopping and baking to do and cards to send and packages to wrap, and she wanted to enjoy every bit of it—to lose herself in her efforts to make this the best Christmas ever. Anna remembered how her mother had loved Christmas and how she'd always strived to make things perfect. That's what Anna wanted this year. Still, she knew she needed to pace herself. And, like she'd promised herself earlier, she would keep her health at the forefront. She would try to eat healthier and get in a little exercise and plenty of rest.

⚬

On Wednesday, Anna studied her image in the mirror. She really did look like Mom. Not just her petite frame and prematurely gray hair, but the color of her eyes and the dark shadows beneath them, the structure of her cheekbones and the beginning signs of hollowness in her cheeks. This was how Mom had looked during the last year of her life. Still, Anna felt determined to fight. She might be dying, but she could do it gracefully. Couldn't she? For one thing, she hadn't had a proper haircut in ages. Lately she'd taken to pulling her shoulder-length hair back in a barrette. Unfortunately this only made her look older.

Anna found the envelope in which she was keeping the leftover money from the sale of her dishes. She pulled it out from her underwear drawer and counted the bills inside. She'd already paid for the engine, giving David the cash so he could use a charge card, which he seemed to appreciate since he was low on cash. And then she'd given him the amount to purchase a gift certificate from British Motors, which was also safe in her underwear drawer, along with the picture of the new engine. She still had a fair amount of money left, and some was already budgeted for gifts for her family. But she decided it would not only be acceptable to use some of it to improve her appearance, it would also be wise. Meredith had already guessed Anna's secret just by looking at her. How many others would begin to be suspicious? Besides that, Michael would probably appreciate her improved appearance.

Anna made an appointment for a "holiday mini-makeover" for Friday morning. She felt a flutter of excitement as she hung up the phone. That would be just six days before Christmas and just in time for the Christmas party that Grant and Suzy were hosting on Saturday night. And perhaps she'd even get something new to wear. Oh, wouldn't Michael be pleased when he saw her? In the meantime, she would finish the other holiday chores on her list—and make sure she got plenty of rest.

Meredith had called a couple of times during the week, but Anna had managed to "miss" those calls, and she'd managed to "forget" to return them. But on Friday morning, just as she was getting ready to leave for her mini-makeover, she saw her sister's white minivan pulling up in front of the house.

"Meredith," Anna called. "So good to see you. I'm on my way to an appointment right now, but maybe we could meet up later—are you off today?"

"Yes," Meri said as she came closer and peered into Anna's eyes. "Why haven't you returned my calls?"

"Oh . . . I've been so busy." Then Anna started rattling off a list of all the things she'd been doing.

"But you did see the doctor?"

"I made an appointment."

Meredith brightened. "Is that where you're going now?"

"Well, I am going to an appointment." Anna glanced away.

"To the doctor?"

"Not today." Anna smiled. "Today I'm having a holiday mini-makeover at La Bella. Hey, why don't you come along? Maybe they can squeeze you in."

"What about the doctor?"

"I made the appointment," Anna said. "But really, I have to run or I'll be late." She unlocked her car. "Sorry."

"Why don't we meet up for lunch?" Meredith suggested. "When will you be done?"

"Around one, I'm guessing."

"Okay, meet me at 1:30 at Renaldo's. It's just a block down from La Bella."

"Sounds great." Anna got in her car and wondered how she'd be able to get her sister off her case about the doctor appointment. Perhaps her best defense would be to fake it. Act as if she was feeling better. And, really, wasn't she? She'd managed to eat and hold down a whole bowl of oatmeal this morning. That was something.

⌘

"So what would you like to do?" Veronica asked as she turned Anna around in the chair to look at her reflection.

"I look pretty bad, don't I?"

"You look a little tired."

"Yes, that's the problem. I want to look healthy and happy and ready for some holiday fun."

Veronica laughed. "Don't we all? Well, do you trust me, Anna?"

Anna frowned slightly. "Well . . . yes. Although I have to draw the line at any hair color. I know the gray makes me look older, but my husband actually likes it."

Veronica fingered her hair. "I think it's kind of pretty. But how about if we gave it more sparkle—without using dye?"

"Sounds great."

"Okay." Veronica wrapped the black cape around Anna's shoulders. "Just relax and we'll see what miracles can happen."

Anna did relax. In fact, she closed her eyes and nearly went to sleep as Veronica and a young woman named Fawn took turns working on her. Veronica was in charge of hair, and Fawn gave Anna a facial and then applied makeup.

"Voilà," Fawn said as she spun Anna's chair around again. "Take a look at you."

Anna opened her eyes and peered at her reflection. "Wow, that really is like a miracle." Her hair was cut short and curling prettily around her face. And although the gray was still there, it did have a sparkle to it. She patted it to discover that it even felt good. "And the makeup," she said. "It looks so soft and natural. And yet it looks fantastic." She turned to Fawn. "But how will I accomplish this again?"

Fawn grinned and handed her a DVD. "That's part of our makeover package. We record what we did so you can do it again at home."

"Of course, you'll need the products," Veronica pointed out. She handed Anna a list. "Everything we used on you is available right here in the salon."

"Thank you," Anna said, looking back at her reflection again. "Really, I think I look ten years younger. Well, except for the gray."

"You look beautiful," Veronica said.

"Absolutely," Fawn agreed. "And that dusky violet on your eyes is stunning. If nothing else, I recommend you get that one."

"That and the hair product," Veronica said as she pointed to an item on the list. "See how your gray hair looks silvery and shimmers? Very pretty."

"And the lip color," Fawn added. "You have to get that too."

Anna laughed. "I might just have to get it all."

She thanked them and went over to see the products and review her list. Although it would've been fun to get all the products, her usual frugality kicked in when she saw the staggering total. So she limited herself to a hundred dollars' worth of beauty products. And to be fair, that was far more than she'd ever spent before. When it was all said and done, Anna knew it had been an extravagant morning, but she thought it was worth it. And she couldn't wait to see what her sister's reaction would be.

"Wow, Anna," Meredith said when they met in the foyer of Renaldo's. "You look fantastic."

Anna patted her hair as the hostess led them to a table. "I feel great too. Really, I wish you'd come with me. It was such fun."

"Maybe I'll make myself an appointment too." Meredith frowned now. "Well, not until after Christmas. Sometime before New Year's though."

"Meaning you have a date planned for New Year's?" As much as Anna didn't want to encourage Meri about this, and as much as she didn't want to hear any more about Cooper,

Anna thought the question might distract her sister from pestering her about seeing the doctor.

"I might."

"So, you're still certain about this thing?"

"The way you say 'this thing,' Anna—it's like you're talking about polio . . . or cancer."

"I'm sorry," Anna said as the hostess filled their water glasses. "I'm trying to be understanding . . . really, I am." She waited for the hostess to leave. "But I still don't see how divorcing Todd is going to make you happy."

Meredith let out a long sigh and picked up her water glass. "That's because you are not me, Anna. If you had to live my life for just one day—twenty-four hours—you might get it."

"I suppose . . ."

"It's not easy living in a loveless marriage. It's even harder when you have a child together."

"But didn't you used to love Todd?" Anna peered at her sister.

"I don't even know. Sometimes I think I just married him because it seemed the thing to do. Everyone else was married. I was done with college." She shrugged. "Planning a wedding sounded like fun." She pointed a finger at Anna. "And you acted like it was so great."

"So great?"

"You know, getting married, having a wedding, possibly starting a family."

"You were talking about your biological clock then," Anna pointed out.

"I was only thirty." Meredith shook her head. "I think I was being influenced by you and your biological clock. I should've waited."

"But you were thirty-four when you had Jackson. Just how long would you have waited?"

122

"I don't know . . . long enough to have met Cooper, I guess."

Anna felt bad now, like maybe this was partially her fault. "How long have you known Cooper?"

"Three years."

"Oh . . ." Anna realized that was only a year less than Meredith had been married.

"I'm not trying to blame you," Meredith said.

Just then the waiter came to take their order, and Anna, thankful for the interruption, quickly perused the menu before settling on soup and salad. Somehow she ought to be able to get that down.

"I'd like the house dressing," she told him. "On the side."

"Certainly." Then he turned to take Meredith's order.

"How's Jackson doing?" Anna asked after the waiter left.

"He's fine. At the sitter's."

Anna wanted to question this but picked up a piece of bread instead. Then, taking her time, she pretended to butter it and slowly broke off a small piece and took a cautious bite. Bread wasn't usually a problem, but just sitting in the restaurant and smelling the various foods was making her feel a little queasy.

"How are you feeling?" Meri asked.

Anna looked up and smiled. "Great."

"Really?"

"Absolutely. I think all I needed was some rest. And my energy is coming back." She started listing off all the things she'd been doing this week, not mentioning the naps or occasional stomachaches.

"That's great," Meredith said. "I was starting to get worried when you didn't call."

"Sorry. I meant to, but it's funny how you can waste more

time when you have it. I can hardly believe a whole week of Christmas break has gone by already."

"Or that there are only five more shopping days until Christmas."

"You're still shopping?"

"Not really, but I just heard that on the radio." Meredith buttered a piece of bread. "Hey, Todd mentioned seeing Michael on campus Wednesday night."

"Huh?" Anna frowned. "On campus?"

"Yeah. Todd had popped into the Night Owl to meet his brother, and—"

"The Night Owl?" Anna shook her head.

"Yeah, I thought that sounded kind of weird too. Why would Michael be on campus and hanging out at the Night Owl?"

"Michael was working Wednesday night," Anna pointed out. "Maybe Todd mistook someone else for him."

"No, he was certain it was Michael."

"Well, maybe he was meeting someone for something work related."

"At the Night Owl?"

"We used to go there for coffee sometimes," Anna said defensively. "It's not just a bar, you know. Lots of students hang out there."

"Yeah, but Michael's not a student."

"Well, maybe it wasn't Michael." Anna stopped talking as the waiter brought their food, but all she could think about was what her husband was doing at a college hangout on a Wednesday night when he was supposed to be working.

"Hey, I didn't mean to upset you," Meredith said as she forked into her Cobb salad.

"I'm not upset."

"I just thought it was weird."

Anna nodded and took a cautious taste of the pumpkin soup. Not bad.

"You guys aren't having problems, are you, Anna?"

"No, of course not."

Meredith pointed her fork accusingly at her. Anna wanted to remind her that it was bad manners to point eating utensils at others, but she didn't. "Anna, I remember you saying something about Michael having a midlife crisis once."

"Oh, I was probably just joking."

"You didn't seem like you were joking."

"Well . . ."

"And then, the other day, when I thought Michael was acting weird with me, you said if he was acting weird, it was probably toward you. What was up with that?"

"Nothing, Meredith." And then, in a last-ditch effort to distract her sister, Anna asked Meredith to tell her more about Cooper. "I've been curious," she said. "What's he really like—and what makes you so attracted to him?"

Naturally this got Meredith going, and soon their lunches were eaten, or mostly, and suddenly Meri was urging Anna to check out a sale at a new boutique a couple of doors down. "I saw the sale sign, and the things I spotted in the window were totally amazing." She smiled at Anna. "And you look so hot with your new makeover, we really should get you something fun to wear for Christmas."

Anna admitted that she had been thinking the same thing, and before long she and Meri were in the boutique trying on all kinds of things.

"You have to get that," Meredith said as Anna modeled a garnet-colored dress. "It is so awesome on you—you look totally hot. Michael is going to have a meltdown when he sees you."

"But it's too expensive," Anna protested.

"It's 30 percent off," the saleswoman said.

"It's still too much," Anna said. Even with the reduction, this dress was still more than $150. And she'd already spent more than she planned with the makeover this morning.

"Fine! Just take it off then. Let's get out of here. I need to pick up Jackson now anyway."

Anna blinked, then returned to the dressing room where she carefully removed the pretty dress. It really was stunning—and surprisingly sexy too. But still it was too much. And yet she hated for Meri to be mad at her. Perhaps she could smooth it over.

"I'll find something at Ross," she whispered to her sister as she hung the dress back on the rack.

"The heck you will," Meri said as she snatched up the dress. "I'm getting this for you, Anna."

"No," Anna said as she chased Meredith to the cashier. "You can't. It's too much."

"No, it's not," Meredith said. Then she turned and actually smiled. "Merry early Christmas, Anna. Now don't look a gift horse in the mouth, okay?"

Anna didn't know what to say, but she also knew it would be pointless to argue with her stubborn younger sister on this. Besides, it was incredibly sweet.

"Well, thank you very much," Anna said as Meredith handed her the sleek silver bag.

"You are very welcome. Now, promise me you'll wear it to the party tomorrow and knock everyone's socks off."

Anna laughed. "I promise you, I most certainly will."

Meri glanced at her watch. "Now I really do need to go pick up Jackson."

They hugged and parted ways, but Anna blinked back tears as she hurried to her car. She wasn't even sure what the source of the tears was this time. Was it Meredith's

126

unexpected generosity? Anna's suppressed fear of cancer? Or was it the startling news that Michael had been seen hanging out with college kids on a night when he was supposedly working late? Anna could not think of one good reason why her husband would be at the Night Owl. But unfortunately she could think of some bad ones.

14

"Okay," Meredith said on the phone. It had been just a couple hours since they'd parted ways downtown, but now Meri had a bee in her bonnet. "You managed to distract me from asking you the exact day and time of this mysterious doctor appointment, Anna. Now I demand to know." Anna muttered the date, and Meredith immediately went ballistic. "No way! You cannot wait that long. That's like a whole stinking month away. Do you know how fast cancer cells can grow in a month? Do you have any idea how much more can be done with early detection these days?"

"But we don't have insurance."

"I don't give a rip about that! Your life is worth more than that, Anna. You cannot wait that long. Do you understand?"

"I can't go in until we have insurance." Anna tried to sound patient, but she wanted to tell her sister to mind her own business.

"Then get insurance. Get it today."

"I don't think that's possible."

"Sure it is, you just pick up the phone and call. Lots of

people do it. You just fill out the forms, let them take your blood pressure and some basic stuff like that. No big deal. Just do it, Anna."

"I can't."

"Why not?"

"I don't want Michael to know what's going on."

"Then don't tell him. Just get a policy for yourself."

"He doesn't live under a stone. He'll figure it out."

"Then just tell him. You'll have to sooner or later anyway."

"I don't want to spoil Christmas."

Now Meredith actually cussed. Anna hadn't heard her younger sister use bad language since they were teens. "Meri," she said in a shocked tone.

"I'm sorry. But you are making me mad. If you don't tell Michael, maybe I will."

"You will not!"

"Yes, I will." Meredith swore again. "And for all we know, Michael has some things he's not telling you, Anna. I mean, what if you're doing this heroic thing, trying to protect Michael, trying to give him some stupid perfect Christmas, and trying to save him a few bucks on insurance—and the whole while he's out there messing around."

"What do you mean?"

"I mean, the writing is on the wall, Anna. You said yourself you were concerned that he might be having a midlife crisis. He works overtime all the time . . . and then he's seen hanging out with college kids at the Night Owl. Use your head, sis."

"Why are you doing this to me, Meri?" Anna felt tears coming again.

"Because I love you. And I refuse to lose you like we lost Mom. You have to see the doctor."

"I will."

"But January 16 is too far out."

"What if I change the date?"

"What if you get insurance today?" Meri said. "And what if you make an appointment for Monday?"

Anna swallowed hard. She knew she couldn't do that. She wouldn't do that.

"Or what if I tell Michael?"

Anna was angry now. "I trusted you!"

"And I'm glad you did. Someone needs to watch out for you."

"Listen, Meredith." Anna's voice was steely calm. "If you tell Michael, I swear to you, I will tell Todd."

"You wouldn't."

"Do you want to try me?" Anna cleared her throat. "Imagine what a lovely Christmas we can all have with everyone hurt and mad and—"

"Fine! You win."

"So you won't tell Michael?"

"No. Christmas is less than a week away. But I swear to you, Anna, if you haven't told him by December 26, I will."

"Fine! And I'll do the same with Todd for you."

"You won't need to," Meredith said. "I'll tell him myself." And then she hung up.

Anna felt sick to her stomach again, but she knew it was probably as related to emotions as anything. And, to be fair, would she act any different toward Meredith if the tables were turned? What if Meri was sick and refusing to see a doctor? But Anna didn't want to think about that. All she wanted was some lukewarm, watered-down ginger ale and a nice long nap.

She had just fallen asleep when the phone rang again. This time it was Michael. "Hi, sweetie," he said.

"Hi."

"Did I wake you?"

"Yeah."

"Sorry about that. And you're probably going to guess what I'm about to tell you," he said.

"Working late again?"

"Yeah. But this will be the last night for a while."

She thought about the Night Owl but didn't say anything.

"Really," he said. "No more overtime until after Christmas."

"Right . . ."

"I'm sorry, really."

"That's okay. I'm pretty tired anyway . . . it's been a long day."

"We'll make up for it tomorrow night, okay? And don't forget it's Grant and Suzy's annual Christmas party."

"Yes . . . I remember." Anna looked at the pretty red dress hanging on the door of her closet and sighed.

The next day, Michael acted perfectly normal. Not only did he rave about her new haircut, but he fixed blueberry pancakes for breakfast as well. But as Anna picked at hers, she wondered if this was some sort of guilt offering. Then he cleaned up the breakfast things and took Huntley for a walk, which only seemed to prove her theory. Why else would he be so nice? Then, shortly after Michael left, her dad called.

"Is everything okay with you?" she asked. They'd already covered the perfunctory hellos, but she was worried now. Her dad didn't usually just call like this—straight out of the blue—without a reason.

"Yeah, sure, I'm fine," he told her. "I just had to run to town this morning—doing a little Christmas shopping for

Donna, you know how that goes—and I thought maybe my oldest child would like to meet me for coffee."

"Meet you for coffee?" She tried not to sound too shocked, but this was so out of character for Dad. She hoped he was okay.

"Yeah. I thought we could meet at Hole in One, you know, get a donut and coffee . . . maybe you have some ideas for Donna's Christmas present. You know how I usually don't get it right."

"Well, sure, Dad. That sounds great. When were you thinking?"

"How about ten thirty?"

"Sounds great." She said good-bye and hung up, but as she got ready to go, she couldn't help but think this was very strange. And the most obvious reason for this unexpected coffee date had to be Dad's health. She wondered if he'd gotten some bad news . . . something he didn't want to tell Donna about. As she drove downtown, she braced herself. And, as she parked her car and walked over to the little donut shop, she realized that her dreams for "the best Christmas ever" were not only unrealistic, they were becoming down-right impossible.

"Hey there, Anna," Dad said as she came into the donut shop. "Pretty cold out there, isn't it?"

She nodded and unbuttoned her coat. "Do you think it'll snow?"

"Maybe so." He tipped his head toward the glass case filled with pastries. "What will you have?"

Anna picked a plain cake donut and a cup of herbal tea, then they went to sit in a booth. "So, Dad, how's it going?"

He frowned slightly. "Well, I guess that's what I want to ask you."

"Me?"

"Yes, that's why I wanted to meet you today."

"But why? I mean, what do you want to ask me about?"

He shrugged as he wrapped his hands around the coffee mug. "How are you doing, Anna?"

She thought for a moment. "Okay."

"Well, that's not what I hear."

"Huh?" She peered curiously at her dad. His hair, cut in his regular crew-cut style, was completely white now, but his blue eyes still had a youthful twinkle. Except that right now they looked worried.

"I hear that you might have something you need to talk about . . . you know, to your old man."

"Who told you that?"

He pressed his lips together, lifting his brows slightly, as if to suggest he wasn't about to reveal his source.

"Has Meredith been talking to you?"

Again the same look.

"What has she told you, Dad?"

"She just said that I should talk to you."

"About?"

"She wasn't specific, Anna. But she acted like it was serious. She told me that a good parent would step in and do something. I think those were her exact words." But now he looked puzzled. "Problem is, I don't know exactly what I'm supposed to step in and do. You got any ideas?"

"Oh, Dad . . ." Anna sighed. "I think it's really sweet that you wanted to help, but trust me, there's nothing you can do for me. Okay?"

"If you say so." He took a slow sip of coffee, then looked curious again. "If you're sure you don't want to talk about it."

"Remember when Mom died?" she said suddenly.

"Well, yeah, of course."

"There were times when I wanted to talk about things then, Dad. But most of the time you didn't want to. Why was that?"

"I just didn't see the point in dwelling on things."

"Or showing emotion?"

"It's probably just the way I was raised," he said. "Back when I was growing up, men and boys were expected to keep their emotions in check."

"Did you ever cry for Mom?"

He looked down at his coffee and frowned, but he didn't answer. And for some reason that just really irritated her.

"Well, if something happened to me, I'd want Michael to cry," she announced.

"And I'm sure that Michael would cry if something happened to you."

She scowled. "Well, I'm not so sure."

"Why not?" Now Dad looked really concerned.

"Just because . . ."

"But Michael loves you, Anna."

"Did you love Mom?"

"Of course."

"But you didn't cry."

"But Michael is different from me. If anything happened to you, I'm sure he'd feel it deeply. I'm sure he'd cry."

She shook her head and broke off a piece of her donut, holding it in her fingers, trying to decide whether to take a bite or not.

"Just because I didn't cry when your mother died does not mean I didn't love her, Anna. I loved her more than anyone will ever know. And I still miss her today."

Anna looked up in time to see his eyes getting misty. "I'm sorry, Dad," she said quickly. "I'm sure you do."

135

Now he smiled. "You look so much like her, Anna. You two are like two peas in a pod."

"In more ways than you know."

A shadow crossed his face and he cocked his head ever so slightly, but he didn't question her words. He just sat there silently. And Anna wondered if he knew . . . if he suspected. Still, she was determined to keep her secret as long as possible. And she felt furious at Meredith for this lame attempt to spill the beans for her.

"Well, I think you've got Michael all wrong too," Dad said. "If anything ever happened to you, that man would be brokenhearted and beside himself with grief."

"You guys really stick together, don't you?"

"I'm just saying what I know is true."

Anna sighed. So many things that her father didn't understand . . . would probably never understand. She wanted to ask him if he would cry when she died, but she knew that would only complicate things more. Instead she asked him what he planned to get for Donna this year.

"Well, I was thinking about one of those diamond necklaces they keep advertising on TV. You know, the ones with three stones. Every time that ad comes on, I hear her sigh."

"It's an emotional advertisement, Dad. It's supposed to make you sigh."

"I know. But, just the same, I think she'd like one of those necklaces."

"You're probably right. I'm sure she'd love one."

"That settles it then." He grinned and picked up his ball cap. "Thanks for helping me to figure it out."

"Thanks for inviting me here for coffee." She grinned back at him. "Maybe we can do it again sometime."

"Maybe so."

Well, at least Dad's not dying, Anna thought as she

returned to her car. Still, he could be a little dense about some things. But maybe that was good—probably some sort of protective device. Just the same, it was aggravating how easily he stood up for Michael. Like they were in some secret boys' club together—a wink and a handshake and everything's just fine. Her dad was a nice guy, but he really could qualify as the king of denial. Of course, Anna could probably win the crown for queen.

And since everyone seemed so deep into denial these days, maybe she'd just continue to play along. So she acted like everything was just fine all day. She and Michael went through their ordinary Saturday routines, and then, when it was time to get ready for the Christmas party, she took her time to apply the makeup just like the DVD showed her. She fixed her hair and then slipped into the garnet dress.

"Wow," Michael said when he saw her. "You look fantastic, Anna." He slipped his arms around her and pulled her close. "Maybe we should scrap that party and just spend the evening alone?"

She smiled. "Well, that'd be nice. Grant's own partner blowing off the Christmas party."

"Yeah, I guess that's a little rude." He bent down and kissed her, lingering in a way that suggested her suspicions about him were ludicrous. "But we could always come home early."

She laughed as they headed out the door. "Sure . . . why not?"

⁂

Grant and Suzy's parties were always the best. The tradition had started back when Grant and Michael were still at the marketing firm. It was probably due to Suzy's gift for entertaining combined with their lovely hillside home that looked out over the city—they were always the first pick for parties. Not that Anna minded, since their bungalow was pretty small. Plus she knew she didn't have the flare that Suzy did. And Grant and Suzy had a full bar, which always seemed to make a lot of people happy. Sometimes a little too happy, in Anna's opinion.

"You look stunning," Grant said as he handed Anna a glass of something red.

"What's this?" Anna watched as Michael was swept away by an older gentleman, probably a client.

"It's a sweet little cabernet that I thought would go nicely with your beautiful dress." He chuckled. "I know you're a lightweight when it comes to alcohol, but you can just carry it around and look pretty."

She laughed. Grant had not only a sharp artist's eye but a quirky sense of humor too. "Well, thank you. I'll try to wear it well."

"I'm still thinking about that lasagna you brought by the other night." He smacked his lips again. "I told Suzy that we'll have to weasel a dinner invite from you guys."

"Of course," she said. "Consider yourself invited. How about after Christmas though."

"Perfect."

"And you guys won't be so busy then."

"Busy?"

"Well, you've really been putting in a lot of hours these past few weeks."

"Oh." He looked uneasy. "Yes . . ."

"You have to admit, you guys have pulled a lot of late nights."

"It's not easy starting up a new business." Now he glanced across the room. "Speaking of which, here comes Thomas Sanders, one of our newest clients. I better go greet him and make him feel at home."

Anna watched as Grant cut through the crowded room. She could tell by his answer that something was wrong. And she decided to get to the bottom of it. She went to the kitchen to find Suzy speaking to one of the caterers about the crab cakes. "That last bunch wasn't even lukewarm," she told the woman. "They really need to be hot when you put them on the tray."

"Yes. We'll take care of it," the woman promised.

"Oh, Anna," Suzy said. "I haven't even had a chance to say hi to you tonight. You look so great. What have you done with your hair?"

Anna told her about La Bella and the holiday special.

"I think I'll give them a call."

"They're miracle workers."

"Well, you look gorgeous."

"I thought I needed to spruce up for Michael's sake," Anna said in a quiet voice, then chuckled. "You know, the guys have been putting in so many late nights, I thought I might need to compete with this new business."

Suzy's eyebrows lifted, but she just nodded. "Yes, it's been pretty demanding, but it sounds like things are really coming along well."

"Yes, Michael has assured me that he won't be putting in any more late nights after Christmas."

Suzy looked truly concerned now. She leaned forward and spoke quietly. "So, has Michael been working late a lot?"

Anna nodded. "Yes, about three nights a week. And sometimes on weekends too."

"Really?" Suzy's brow creased.

"Do you mean that Grant hasn't been?"

"Oh, he works late occasionally. But not three nights a week. I don't think I could stand for that."

"Especially with the demands of your job. I heard that you might be made partner at the law firm before next year."

Suzy smiled. "Well, I don't believe in counting my chickens too soon, but it is looking good."

Anna patted her on the back. "Congratulations. I'm sure you deserve it." Then Anna excused herself to the powder room, which she really did need to use. But once there, it took all of her self-control not to break into tears. Instead, she pulled out her cell phone and called her sister.

"Hey, what's up?" Meredith asked. "I thought maybe you weren't speaking to me."

"You mean after you set Dad on me today?"

"How'd that go?"

"I'll tell you later—" Anna's voice broke.

"What's wrong?"

"Just—just everything," she sobbed. Then she poured out all that she'd just learned and begged Meredith to come rescue her from the party.

"Sure," Meri said. "Jackson's already in bed and Todd is parked in front of the TV. I'll be right over."

"I'll meet you on the street," Anna said. "I think I can sneak out the back door."

"Okay. Give me ten minutes."

"Thanks."

15

After making a smooth getaway, Anna reassured her sister that she would be fine at home by herself. And after she changed into her pajamas and calmed herself with a glass of warm milk, she wondered if she hadn't simply overreacted to everything. The truth was, she had no proof that Michael was cheating on her. Naturally Meredith assumed that was the only possible explanation. And Anna had to admit it didn't look good. But then Anna remembered Michael's tenderness toward her earlier that evening. The sweet way he'd walked her into the party.

Anna turned and looked at the clock. The party! It was after ten now, and Michael was probably looking for her. She grabbed the phone and called his cell. It wasn't turned on, but she left a message anyway.

"I'm sorry," she said. "But I got sick to my stomach at the party. I could see you were having a good time, so I called and asked Meri to pick me up. I'm at home now and feeling better. Please, don't worry about me and stay as long as you like. Bye." *There*, she thought, *that should smooth this over.*

At least for the time being. She had no idea what she'd say to him tomorrow.

But tomorrow came, and Michael, other than being concerned for her health, seemed perfectly normal. But as they were driving home from church, his cell phone rang, and she listened as he talked. It sounded like he was talking to Grant, but she couldn't be sure. And it sounded as if he was going to leave for a business trip, maybe even by tomorrow.

"Are you sure it can't wait until after Christmas?" he asked, then waited. "No, I understand. And no more than two days? You're positive?" He sighed. "Okay. No, it's fine. I don't mind." Now he chuckled. "Well, that would be great. Let's hope so." Then he closed his phone and slipped it back into his blazer pocket.

"Was that Grant?"

"Yes. We have a big account that we've been working on, and they're about to make up their mind. But Grant says if one of us doesn't go up to Seattle, we won't have a chance."

"Why doesn't he go?"

"It's Martha's Christmas ballet tomorrow night."

"Wow, they scheduled that pretty close to Christmas."

"You know how crazy schedules get. Anyway, he can't miss it."

"So you're going to Seattle?"

"Yes."

"Hey, maybe I could go too?"

He turned and glanced at her. "You could . . . but I'll mostly be in meetings. And airfare at this late notice, and during the holidays, well, it won't be cheap. Plus it'll be a madhouse at the airports. You really want to subject yourself to that?"

"I guess not."

"And you said you weren't feeling well last night. What

142

if you're coming down with something? It'd be a drag to be sick for Christmas."

She sighed. "I suppose so . . ." Then she tried not to imagine some pretty college ingenue flying up to Seattle with him, snuggled together in the plane, holding hands, sharing a blanket. She tried not to think of some swanky city hotel and the cool restaurant where the two of them would sit, head to head, laughing about how they had pulled off this little holiday rendezvous. She knew she was being ridiculous.

As it turned out, Michael left that evening. That way he would be there first thing in the morning, ready to make his presentation and schmooze as needed. "I'll just leave the car at the airport," he had told her as he packed his bags. "It's only for two nights."

Two nights . . . what could happen in two nights? What had already happened? But she hadn't voiced these fears, she had simply nodded and said that it sounded like a good plan. But when he kissed her good-bye, she held back. He assumed it was because she felt left out, and he promised to make good when he came home on Tuesday night. "And don't forget," he reminded her. "You said this was going to be the best Christmas ever, Anna."

How could she forget? Those words would probably come back to haunt her for—for how long? Realistically, it probably would be only a matter of months . . . certainly not years. If anything, her longing for a perfect Christmas could haunt Michael for years. Who knew what his next Christmas would be like? But then again, perhaps it would be a relief for him. It would make everything so much simpler. He would be the sad widower. And Dad was right, Michael probably would cry. It would seem unnatural if he didn't. And he'd probably wait an appropriate amount of time before he remarried his new young love. She tried to imagine next Christmas.

Meredith would probably be married to this mysterious Cooper by then. And Michael would probably bring his new girlfriend. How different things would be in just one year.

For two long days, Anna tormented herself with these thoughts. She also did all the things that she figured a wife who suspected her husband of cheating might do. She went through drawers and pockets, and checked bills and receipts and phone records. But really she didn't find anything very questionable. There seemed to be only two distinct possibilities: (1) Michael was an expert at hiding his trail, or (2) Michael was innocent. By Tuesday afternoon, she decided—after much prayer—to do her best to accept option two. She even planned a nice dinner for him—a welcome home. And while they ate dinner, she would confess to him all that she had heard and her concerns. And he, naturally, would explain everything. And then, somehow, they would make the most of Christmas.

Of course, by now her expectation level for the holiday had diminished greatly. Despite the fact that snow was beginning to fly, she knew that this Christmas wouldn't be the perfect one she'd dreamed of. For one thing, the car engine had not arrived, and at this rate, she knew it was totally impossible to have it installed by Christmas even if it did get here. Still, she had her placeholder gift all ready for Michael. She'd found a very cool card with a picture on the front of an MG that looked a lot like his, and she'd put the gift certificate and the picture of the engine inside. And the mechanic was scheduled for the following week, and according to David, it was highly likely that the car would be running by New Year's Eve. That seemed the best she could do now. And, to be honest, there was a part of her that had ceased to care. And . . . she missed her dishes.

As Anna organized things for the dinner she planned to

serve on Christmas for some of her family, including her neighbor Bernice, she longed for a fine set of china to serve it on. She tried not to imagine her elegant Meissen set on Loraine's table, and, although she knew it would look beautiful, she also knew she would feel jealous to see other people using it. And she knew it was immature and selfish, but she wished that china was still hers.

So what if it had been stored in crates. And so what if it didn't go with the style of their house . . . she had loved it anyway. And now she missed it desperately. Even so, she knew that it was worth the exchange. She knew she'd done the right thing. What good would those dishes be after she was gone anyway? No one but a person like Loraine would appreciate them like Anna had. And at least Michael would have his car—and hopefully some happy memories to go with it. Wasn't that worth it?

Anna set the table with her everyday dishes, which were actually very nice. She had everything ready to go for Michael's welcome-home dinner when she noticed the snow coming down harder now. She also noticed that Huntley was antsy, just like her second graders would be under the same circumstances. Her old beagle knew there was some exciting weather going on outside, and he needed to check it out. "You want to go for a walk?" she asked, and he wagged his tail. "Okay, just a quick one . . . long enough for you to taste some snow." She put on her heavy coat, wrapped a scarf around her head and neck, and shoved her feet into her boots, and they were ready to go.

It really was beautiful out. The sky had a dusky purple cast to it, and the snowflakes illuminated in the streetlights were tumbling down. Huntley sniffed at the snow and even bit at some of the falling flakes, and Anna simply looked up in wonder. They really were going to have a white Christmas after all. Maybe she had given up too soon. Maybe this really was going to be the best Christmas ever. She walked along happily, admiring how ordinary things like cars and houses and trees took on a completely new and wonderful appearance with a fine white coat of snow. Maybe that was like forgiveness . . . or how love covered a multitude of sins. Maybe that's how she needed to see Michael tonight. Not that he had even sinned. She didn't know that for sure. And the more she thought about it, the less likely it seemed. Still, she decided as she walked back to the house, if he had sinned, she would choose to forgive him. Oh, definitely, she'd need God's help. But she would do her best to forgive him. And, really, she'd wanted to give him the best Christmas present ever . . . what could be better than forgiveness?

As she turned the corner to their house, she hoped that Michael's car would be parked out front. His flight should've gotten in by now. But the street was empty and white. She shook the snow off her coat and scarf and brushed it from Huntley's back, then went inside to see that the message light on the phone was flashing. She pushed the message button and listened.

"Anna," a crackly voice that sounded like Michael said. "I'm stuck at Sea-Tac right now. All the flights are delayed thanks to this winter storm. I'm trying to get out, but it's not looking good. I may be stuck in Seattle until morning. I'd call you on my cell, but it was dead when I got to the airport. I'll try to find an outlet to charge it. But this place is a madhouse. Just be thankful you're not here, sweetie. Talk to you later."

Later, when Anna didn't hear back from him, she tried to call his cell but only got his voicemail. So she told him she missed him and she loved him and to take care, and then she cried herself to sleep. She knew that she was being silly and melodramatic and that things would probably look much better in the morning, but she just couldn't help herself. It all seemed so hopeless. She wondered why she even tried. And when she attempted to pray, she felt like every ounce of faith had already been spent. It wasn't that she'd given up on God, but she just didn't have the energy or the words to hold on anymore. Hopefully he was holding on to her.

16

As it turned out, things did look better in the morning. Not only was the sun shining down on about four inches of crisp, white snow, but David called to announce that Michael's engine had arrived last night. "It's at British Motors right now," he told her. "Ron said that it's a beauty."

"Really?" she cried. "That's awesome."

"I was thinking that I could pick up the car when you guys are heading over to Dad's tonight."

"You don't mind?"

"No, I'm having fun with this. Besides, I'm earning my chance to take it out for a spin, right?"

"Of course."

"So, I thought I could drop Celeste at Dad and Donna's and then make an excuse to run some errand. By then you guys will be on your way, and Ron will meet me to trailer it up."

"He doesn't mind?"

"He thinks what you're doing is so cool, Anna. In fact, he can't wait to meet you."

"Really?"

"Yeah. Just make sure you leave the garage door unlocked, okay?"

"No problem. We never lock it anyway."

"Michael is going to be so jazzed."

"That is, if he gets home."

"Huh?"

She explained about the weather and cancellations.

"Oh, yeah, I heard the storm really messed with some West Coast flights."

"I haven't heard from him this morning," she said.

"Maybe that means he's on his way."

"Maybe . . ."

"Well, whenever he does get here, he's gonna love his Christmas present, Anna. You can count on that."

"I hope so."

When Michael finally did call, it was past noon. "It looks like the flight is going to go," he told her. "I would've called you sooner, but I wanted to wait until I was sure. We've been sitting on this plane since 8:30."

"You're kidding."

"Nope. And it's getting old. But I should be home around three . . . well, maybe four by the time I get out of the airport."

"Dad's expecting everyone at six."

"I'm looking forward to it."

"I love you, Michael," she said, feeling a little uncertain . . . as if he might not feel the same way about her anymore.

"I love you too, Anna. I can't wait to wish you Merry Christmas."

"Me too. Fly safely."

Anna hung up and, as usual, whispered a prayer for his safe return home. That struck her as slightly ironic, because she'd always been the one to fret over airline safety, worrying that his flight would go down and she would lose him. She was always on pins and needles when he traveled, particularly if it was a cross-country flight. How many times had she endured the anxiety of Michael being taken from her? How many times had she prayed? And now everything felt different. He would be the one left to deal with losing her.

Anna distracted herself by getting things ready for the Christmas dinner tomorrow. She lined up the dry ingredients for turkey dressing—all ready to go. She even made the Jell-O salad that her dad so loved but everyone else made jokes about. Then, with the kitchen prepped for tomorrow, she busied herself by bagging and boxing the Christmas presents she'd gotten for her family, pausing to examine her meticulously wrapped gifts, knowing full well that the pretty packages would simply be torn open, the paper and ribbons tossed aside. But she had enjoyed putting them together, carefully choosing the type of wrapping paper that suited each member of her family. In her mind, the gifts were perfect—inside and out. She just hoped her relatives would appreciate them.

Then she put on her parka and loaded everything into her car. It took several trips, and each time she went out, Huntley gave her that look—that "why can't I go outside too?" look. "Later," she told him. "I'm sure your papa will take you out." This way she felt assured that, even if Michael got home in the nick of time, everything would be ready to go. The main thing was to get out of there before David and Ron came to pick up the car.

Finally, she put the finishing touches on the enormous fruit salad she was taking for tonight's buffet and put together an attractive plate of homemade cookies to share with Dad and Donna. She'd already taken cookie plates to her neighbors, including Bernice across the street, reminding her that they expected her to join them for Christmas Day tomorrow. Bernice had promised to "be there with bells on."

Michael made it home just in time to dump his bags, grab a shower, and make some quick phone calls, which she hoped were business related but couldn't be certain, since she couldn't hear him as he talked on his cell phone in the bathroom. *Stop being so suspicious*, she told herself as she fed Huntley and filled his water dish, promising him a walk tomorrow morning. Then she gave him a new rawhide bone. "Merry Christmas, old boy," she said as she scratched him behind the ear.

"Ready to go?" Michael said.

"Yes, I already loaded everything in my car."

"Such a smart woman." Then he hugged and kissed her in such a way that she felt certain that her suspicions about another woman must be wrong. Either that or her husband deserved an Oscar for his performance.

She handed him her car keys. "Want to drive?"

"Sure. That snow's getting pretty messy in town. I actually slid coming off Arbor Drive. After that I slowed down."

Anna glanced down their street as Michael pulled out. She wondered if David and Ron might be lurking around the corner just waiting for them to go. She also wondered how Michael would react when he found out that it was just a matter of days before his beloved MG was up and running. Suddenly the old excitement of pulling off a great Christmas grabbed her again. She felt like she was about six years old and waiting for Santa to arrive.

"This is so beautiful out here," she gushed as he drove through their neighborhood. "I love snow."

"I do too—at least I do right now. I wasn't too crazy about it when I was stuck in Sea-Tac."

"I guess it was a good thing I didn't go with you after all. Hey, how did your presentation go?"

He grinned. "Pretty well, I think. We won't know until after Christmas. But if we get this account, Anna . . . well, things are really going to change for us."

She nodded. "That's great." Unfortunately the things that she expected to change wouldn't be good things. But Anna didn't want to think about that tonight. She wasn't going to let anything ruin this Christmas.

⌘

"You're here!" Donna said as Anna and Michael came into the house loaded down with packages.

"Not that it matters," Celeste said. "Since everyone else isn't."

"Who's not here?" Anna asked as she handed a bag to Donna and peeled off her coat.

"Your brother," Celeste said. "He just dumped me and took off."

Anna patted Celeste's shoulder. "Sorry about that. But how are you doing? How's baby?"

Celeste brightened. "I'm okay, considering. And I finally got some real maternity clothes." She held out her hands to model a form-fitting pale pink maternity top, sticking out her tiny tummy. "See?"

"Pretty."

"And your dad's been missing in action for the past hour," Donna said. "He said he had some last-minute errands to do, but I thought he'd be back by now."

"Well, it is Christmas," Michael said, winking at Donna. "You know how those last-minute errands can be."

"Yeah, he probably forgot to get you a present," Celeste teased.

Donna's face fell. "Oh, good grief," she said. "Surely he's not out there trying to shop tonight."

"I don't think so . . ." Anna said. "And I happen to know a little something about it."

Donna smiled. "Well, sometimes I think we make too much about gifts at Christmastime. One of these years I'm going to call a Christmas truce—no gift exchanging—period."

"Well, not this year," Michael said as he set a bag of gifts beneath the tree.

"Hey, where's Meri?" Anna asked, looking around.

"They're running late," Donna said, "but the grandmas are in the living room watching *White Christmas*."

Celeste feigned a yawn, patting her mouth for drama.

"Need any help in the kitchen?" Anna said, although she happened to like that movie.

"Sure," Donna said. "I never refuse an offer of help."

"Guess I'll go keep the grandmas company," Celeste said.

"And I'll finish unloading the car," Michael said.

Anna chatted with Donna as they worked together in the kitchen. Then the phone rang. "That's probably your dad," Donna said as she picked it up. "Oh, hi, David. What's up? Oh, you want to speak to Anna? Sure. She's right here." She handed the receiver to Anna with a curious expression.

"Anna?" David said. *"Where is the car?"*

"Huh?"

"The MG? Where is it?"

"In the garage, like I said."

"We're *in* the garage right now. The car is not here, Anna."

"What do you mean?"

"I mean *it's not here*. I'm telling you the car is gone."

"It can't be gone." Anna felt sick to her stomach again. She sat down on a stool and tried to understand what was happening. "It has to be there, David."

"Well, it's not. The dustcover is folded neatly in the corner, almost like the car resurrected itself and flew off to car heaven."

"Very funny."

"Do you think someone stole it?"

"Well, we don't lock the door. But the car doesn't run. It's not like anyone could hot-wire it and zip off. We were never worried about thieves."

"Well, you can be worried now."

"This is a total catastrophe."

"I know. So what do I do now?"

"I guess there's nothing you can do, David." Anna sighed. "Just tell Ron I'm sorry to have wasted his time and get yourself back here. After all, it is still Christmas."

"I know, but the car and the engine and what about the—"

"Just let it go for now."

"Okay."

Then Anna hung up and turned to Donna, who now looked extremely curious. "Everything okay?"

Anna just shook her head. "Not exactly."

"Is David having some kind of car troubles?"

"Not exactly," she said again. "More like I'm having car troubles. But I'll explain it all to you later. Okay?" Then Anna went out to speak to Michael, but to her surprise he didn't seem to be around. And when she looked outside, her car was gone too. "Where'd my hubby go?" she asked Celeste.

Celeste just shrugged. "He said he needed to pick up some ice cream."

"Ice cream?"

"Yeah. If you ask me, all these guys are nuttier than Grandma Lily's fruitcake."

"You don't like my fruitcake?" Grandma Lily asked.

Celeste patted her hand. "Of course I do. After all, you spike it with rum, don't you?"

Giving up on Michael, Anna returned to the kitchen to help Donna. And as they worked, she relieved Donna's curiosity by explaining about Michael's MG and her grand plan to give him the best Christmas gift ever. "Please don't tell anyone though. Not yet anyway," she said. "Not until we figure this out."

"So you really don't know where the car went?" Donna asked.

"No, I don't have a clue. Hopefully it's not stolen. Who would steal a car that doesn't even run?"

"When did you last see the car?"

Anna shrugged. "Goodness, I don't know. I hardly ever go out to the garage."

"Poor Michael."

"Yes, not only does this ruin his present, but he's also out a very sweet car. He loved that car, Donna."

"Are you going to tell him tonight?"

"I don't know. Maybe not until we get home, or maybe even not until after Christmas. No need to spoil his evening. He was in such good spirits. Although I don't know why he went out to get ice cream like that."

"Maybe he's having a rendezvous with your dad." Donna shook her head. "I can't figure out what got into Kenneth, taking off like that."

"Yeah, and I thought Dad said we were eating at six o'clock sharp." She pointed to the clock.

"He did." Donna frowned. "And it's nearly seven. But I can't get mad just at your dad. Not with most of the menfolk AWOL right now."

"Well, it sounds like Meri and Todd just got here," Anna said. "I can hear Jackson running down the hallway."

Donna glanced out the kitchen window. "Oh, good. And that looks like your dad's pickup pulling up right now."

Before long, all the missing players were present and accounted for, and after Dad said a sweet Christmas blessing, they all lined up for the buffet dinner.

"This looks totally great, Donna," Meredith said as she took a generous serving of mashed potatoes. "Thanks for going to all this effort."

"Yeah," Michael said. "After scrounging on airport food for twenty-four hours, I can't wait to sink my teeth into a slice of that ham."

"Did you really spend the night in the airport?" David asked.

"I did."

"Seriously?" Meri said. "What did you do? Sleep on the floor?"

"Yuck," Celeste said. "Can you imagine the cooties?"

"The airlines actually brought us some of those flimsy blankets and pillows." Michael laughed. "Like that made everything so much better."

"You must be exhausted," Todd said.

"I'm looking forward to my own bed tonight." Michael winked at Anna, but at the same time, Anna felt Meredith jabbing her with her fork. Anna glared at her sister, but Meri just smirked like she still thought Michael was guilty.

Anna felt torn as the evening wore on. On one hand, she had no desire to break the news of the missing car to Michael. But on the other hand, she felt totally drained. Her last hope of making this Christmas special seemed to have totally evaporated with David's phone call. She knew that Christmas should be about more than just giving gifts. But she couldn't believe that she'd sacrificed Great-Gran's Meissen china for—for what? An expensive engine that was no longer needed and a gift certificate that could never be used? Or perhaps Michael's car wasn't gone for good. Maybe Michael had sent it out for something—like a new paint job? Oh, she knew that was ridiculous. But she wasn't quite ready to give up. Not yet.

Finally, the food was eaten or put away, the packages had been opened with wrappings still strewn all over the floor, polite thank-yous had been exchanged whether or not they were sincere, old familiar carols had been sung with gusto while Donna played the piano, and eventually everyone seemed ready to call it a night.

"Your house tomorrow," Donna said to Anna and Michael as she handed them their coats.

"Two o'clock sharp," Michael said in a cheerful voice, and then the two of them wished everyone Merry Christmas and stepped outside into the winter wonderland. Michael slipped an arm around Anna's waist as they went down the snow-cleared walk to the car. "Just to keep you safe," he said as he drew her closer. Then he opened the passenger door, but before he released her, he bent over and kissed her soundly. "Merry Christmas, sweetie."

"Merry Christmas to you too," she murmured back.

Then once they were both in the car he started humming "Jingle Bells."

"You're certainly in a good mood," she said, knowing full well that she would ruin his happy spirits once she informed him of the missing MG.

"I certainly am."

"Is it just Christmas in general?"

"Maybe . . ." He turned and grinned at her. "Or maybe it's because I have a special Christmas present waiting for you at home."

She tried to look pleased with this announcement, but all

she could think of was that she had nothing for him. Nothing he would want anyway. Nothing but a mess she still had to unravel. Could engines be returned?

When they got home, Michael told her she had to close her eyes as they went into the house, so she complied. Then he walked her through the living room, until they finally stopped in what she knew must be the dining room. "Okay to look now," he said. "Merry Christmas, Anna!"

She opened her eyes and was stunned to see a gorgeous set of dining room furniture in front of her. A long, rectangular table with eight marvelous chairs. "Oh, Michael," she gushed as she ran a hand over the smooth surface of the table. "It's Craftsman style . . . and it's absolutely perfect."

"It's Stickley."

"No way!"

"The table and chairs anyway." He nodded over to a china cabinet that was against the wall. "That's not."

"Oh!" she cried. "I didn't even see that. Oh, it's so beautiful. But how can we afford these pieces? They must've cost a fortune, and we promised not to go into more debt."

"No new debt has been incurred, my love."

"Did you win some lottery then?"

"Nope." He grinned even bigger.

"Oh, Michael, it's all so beautiful. I don't know what to say." She threw her arms around him and broke into tears.

"Well, don't cry, sweetie. Or are those tears of happiness?"

"I'm just so shocked. How could you possibly afford this?"

"Well, I couldn't afford the whole set. I figured out a way to pay for the table and chairs after I found them at Emery's Fine Furniture—but it was the china cabinet that I really wanted, and it was a small fortune. But remember how I've always wanted to learn woodworking?"

She nodded, wiping tears from her cheeks with the backs of her hands.

"Well, there was a night class at the college last semester. I signed up, and the next thing you know, I was building this Craftsman-style china cabinet."

Anna felt dizzy now, like the dining room was starting to spin. She sat down in a chair and stared up at the magnificent cabinet. "You built this?"

He smiled proudly. "I did. With the help of a master. Joe Farnsworth."

"I've heard of him."

"He taught the class and really helped me a lot with my project. But I didn't want you to know what I was up to, so I kept pretending to be working late. I hated lying to you, Anna, but I wanted this to be a surprise."

She nodded, taking in a deep breath. "It's a huge surprise. And I love it. But I have to know . . . how *did* you pay for everything?"

He shrugged. "Well, you know, the old MG was just sitting there in the garage and—"

"No way!" Anna shot to her feet. "You sold your car?"

"I didn't think you'd mind. I mean, it was just gathering dust and—"

"No!" Anna waved her hand in front of him, trying to stop his words.

"What's wrong?"

"Just a minute," she told him, turning to dash to the bedroom. "Let me get your present for you now." Within seconds, she returned with her envelope, waiting with a pounding heart as he opened it . . . watching as he examined the card, the photo, the gift certificate . . . and seeing realization set in.

He looked at her with a creased forehead and misty eyes. "Anna, Anna . . . what did you do?"

"I bought you an engine," she said. And suddenly she was starting to chuckle. "And I was going to get it put in your car." She giggled a bit more as she pointed to the gift certificate. "And I wanted it all done by Christmas, but it didn't work out. Then David came over here this evening to get the car, and—" She burst out into loud laughter now. "And it wasn't here! He called me at Dad's and we were both so upset and I thought it had been stolen and it's—you—you sold it!" She realized she probably sounded hysterical as she continued to laugh. But Michael just gathered her up into his arms.

"I can't believe you," he said softly. "But I have a question for you now. We promised no more debt, Anna. How could you possibly pay for an engine as well as this gift certificate?"

"My china," she whispered, glancing at the empty cabinet. "I sold it."

"You sold it?" Michael held her back and stared down at her. "But you loved that china. It was Great-Gran's. It's the reason I made you the china cabinet."

She nodded. "I know, I know. But I love you way more than the china, Michael. I did it for you."

"I cannot believe how blessed I am," he said as he wrapped an arm around her waist.

She looked up at the beautiful cabinet again and sighed. "I can't believe you made that for me, Michael." She thought of all her suspicions and felt terrible. How could she have been so wrong? How she had misjudged him. And the whole time he was doing this for her.

Michael shook his head. "I can't believe you have no beautiful china to put inside of it now."

"I'm sorry."

"You should've seen your dad and me running all over the house, searching for your china. I was fit to be tied."

"Dad was in on this?"

"Yep. He helped to get the stuff delivered here, and then I sneaked over to make sure it was all set up okay. I wanted to get some of your china out and put it in the cabinet and on the table, but when I couldn't find it, I figured you must've stored it somewhere. I never dreamed you'd sold it."

"Merry Christmas, Michael."

"Merry Christmas, darling." And then they kissed and they kissed some more. And by the time they said good night a couple of hours later, Anna thought that perhaps this really had been the best Christmas ever.

17

Anna woke to the sound of someone ringing the doorbell—again and again as if their finger was stuck. She glanced at the clock to see that it wasn't even seven yet. And wasn't this a holiday? What was going on?

"Who's that?" Michael said groggily.

"Santa?"

"I'll go see."

Michael took off, and Anna grabbed up her bathrobe, suddenly worried that something might be wrong. Who would possibly be ringing their doorbell at this hour, and on Christmas Day, unless something was terribly wrong?

"Anna," Michael called. "Your sister's here."

"Coming," Anna said. She prepared herself for the worst now. Had Meredith already told Todd the bad news about wanting a divorce? Had Todd gone into a rage and thrown her and Jackson out? What was happening? But when Anna got to the living room, it was only Meri standing there, still wearing her pajamas beneath her ski parka, along with a big grin.

"Meri?" Anna stared at her. "What's going on?"

Meredith held out a plain brown paper bag. "Merry Christmas, Anna banana."

"Huh?" Anna wanted to ask her sister if she'd lost her mind or taken up drinking recently.

"Just a little something for you." Meri winked at her now.

"What?" Michael said, peering to see what was inside of the bag. "Oh, Meri," he said. "That is in totally bad taste. What on earth are you think—"

"It's for Anna, not you." Meredith held the bag toward Anna. "Here, Anna."

So Anna stepped forward, took the bag from her, and looked inside. "Meredith!"

"Let me explain. I just got this—"

"If you think this is funny, it is not." Anna pulled out an all-too-familiar-looking EPT box—the same brand of pregnancy testing kit that she had used while they underwent all those fertility treatments. "This is just plain mean, Meri."

"Seriously, Meredith," Michael said. "You've pulled some stunts in your—"

"Let me explain!"

"Fine," Michael said. "Explain."

Meredith tossed Anna a glance, then stuck her chin out and began. "Anna thinks she has ovarian cancer, Michael."

Michael turned to look at Anna with a shocked expression. "Is that true?"

"I don't actually know . . . I mean, I haven't been to the doctor yet."

"Why not?" He went to her now, put his arm around her shoulders.

"We don't have insurance."

"That doesn't matter. I mean, this is serious. What about your mom?"

164

"Exactly," Meredith said. "That's what I told her."

"I have an appointment," Anna said weakly.

"Well, never mind for now," Meredith said. "Let me explain the kit. I got to thinking, Anna. All the symptoms of ovarian cancer are very similar to pregnancy symptoms—"

"No, Meri," Anna said. "That's not it. I've been pregnant before, and I never felt like this. These are real symptoms and—"

"Wait a minute, will you?" Meredith stood in front of Anna now. "I've been pregnant too, Anna. Remember? And when I got pregnant, I thought I had ovarian cancer at first. I never told you, but I had quite a scare."

"Really?" Anna peered curiously at her. "But my—my last pregnancy . . ." Anna tried to remember. "I never got sick or anything. I felt fine the whole time."

"Every pregnancy is different, Anna."

"I know, but—"

"Think about it, Anna. Feeling bloated, having stomach problems, needing to use the bathroom frequently . . . that's how lots of pregnant women feel."

"But I already took a home pregnancy test, and—"

"When?"

"It doesn't matter. It was negative, Meri."

"Maybe you did something wrong, or maybe it was defective."

Anna considered this. "It was an old kit . . ."

"And I'll bet you only tried it once."

"Yes, but—"

"Okay, Anna, here's what pushed me over the edge. Remember when we were trying on dresses at the boutique?" She pointed her finger at Michael now. "Wasn't Anna something in that red dress?"

He nodded. "Yeah. She looked fantastic."

165

"Exactly! Now, I don't mean to pick on you, Anna. But you've never been terribly well-endowed in the bosom area, and you were like popping out of—"

"Oh my gosh!" Anna screamed, looking down at her fuller-than-usual chest.

Meredith tapped her finger on the box. "Please, Anna. Just go try it. Really, what could it hurt?"

"Besides one more disappointment," Michael said as he pulled Anna closer to him. "You don't have to if you don't want to, sweetie."

"But what if Meri is right?" Anna said. "I mean, she makes a good point."

"Come on," Meredith yelled as she pulled Anna by the arm and off toward the bathroom. "What are you waiting for?"

"Okay, okay." Anna felt a rush of excitement combined with a heavy sense of foreboding. "But let me do it alone, okay?"

"Okay. Just do it."

So Anna went into the bathroom and performed the task as she had so many times before. And, as she waited for the results, she prayed. She didn't ask for a miracle, she simply asked for God's will. And when she checked the testing stick, it was positive. She stared at it in disbelief, then realized there were two more tests in the box, so she decided to try it again. Maybe she'd done something wrong the first time. But the second time showed the same result. Still, she wanted to be certain.

"Everything okay in there?" Meri called.

"Don't bug her," Michael said. "She knows what she's doing."

Without answering, Anna did the test a third time. As she waited she could hear Meri and Michael talking. He was telling her about their strange gift exchange. And finally the third test was done, and it too was positive. She burst out of the bathroom door, running toward them. "Merry Christmas!" she cried. Then she threw her arms around both of them at the same time.

"Are you?" Michael's eyes grew wide.

"I did the test three times," she said. "Just to be sure."

"And?" Meredith grabbed Anna's hand.

"I am pregnant!" she cried. "Merry Christmas!"

And the three of them sang and danced and shouted so loudly that Anna was worried that the neighbors might actually complain. But she didn't even care. Because this truly was, without a doubt, the best Christmas ever!

The Gift of the Magi

The magi, as you know, were wise men—wonderfully wise men—who brought gifts to the Babe in the manger. They invented the art of giving Christmas presents. Being wise, their gifts were no doubt wise ones, possibly bearing the privilege of exchange in case of duplication. And here I have lamely related to you the uneventful chronicle of two foolish children in a flat who most unwisely sacrificed for each other the greatest treasures of their house. But in a last word to the wise of these days let it be said that of all who give gifts these two were the wisest. Of all who give and receive gifts, such as they are wisest. Everywhere they are wisest. They are the magi.

O. Henry

Melody Carlson is the prolific author of more than two hundred books, including fiction, nonfiction, and gift books for adults, young adults, and children. She is also the author of *Three Days, The Gift of Christmas Present, The Christmas Bus,* and *An Irish Christmas.* Her writing has won several awards, including a Gold Medallion for *King of the Stable* (Crossway, 1998) and a Romance Writers of America Rita Award for *Homeward* (Multnomah, 1997). She lives with her husband in Sisters, Oregon. Visit her website at www .melodycarlson.com.